"Let's do this." Eli moved like he always did, with confidence and certainty, heading toward the house without a backward glance.

Not reckless, but with an assuredness Ava rarely had without first prepping a plan and then a backup plan.

She was about ten feet behind him when Lacey started barking, a deep timbre to her voice that startled Ava.

Eli glanced back at them, then whipped forward again. He pointed off to the side and mostly behind the house, where the hint of something man-made was visible among the trees. A shed, Ava realized.

Eli lifted his hands, making the motion of someone running, then took off in a run himself toward that shed.

Lacey kept barking, more frantically now.

Dread hit Ava hard, slamming into her chest with the force of a suspect trying to knock her over. "Eli, *no*!" she screamed at him, even as Lacey overtook her and raced after Eli.

Then the world around her exploded in a deafening blast of heat and fire.

This book is for my niece and nephews, Kalan, Will and Miles, who are constant examples of what it means to be generous, kind and curious. They inspire me every single day as they create their own life stories.

SNIFFING OUT DANGER

Elizabeth Heiter

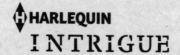

Special thanks and acknowledgment are given to Elizabeth Heiter
for her contribution to the K-9s on Patrol miniseries.

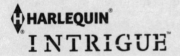

Recycling programs
for this product may
not exist in your area.

ISBN-13: 978-1-335-48955-5

Sniffing Out Danger

Copyright © 2022 by Harlequin Enterprises ULC

For questions and comments about the quality of this book,
please contact us at CustomerService@Harlequin.com.

Harlequin Enterprises ULC
22 Adelaide St. West, 41st Floor
Toronto, Ontario M5H 4E3, Canada
www.Harlequin.com

Printed in U.S.A.

Elizabeth Heiter likes her suspense to feature strong heroines, chilling villains, psychological twists and a little romance. Her research has taken her into the minds of serial killers, through murder investigations and onto the FBI Academy's shooting range. Elizabeth graduated from the University of Michigan with a degree in English literature. She's a member of International Thriller Writers and Romance Writers of America. Visit Elizabeth at www.elizabethheiter.com.

Books by Elizabeth Heiter

Harlequin Intrigue

Sniffing Out Danger

A K-9 Alaska Novel

K-9 Defense
Alaska Mountain Rescue
K-9 Cold Case
K-9 Hideout

The Lawmen: Bullets and Brawn

Bodyguard with a Badge
Police Protector
Secret Agent Surrender

The Lawmen

Disarming Detective
Seduced by the Sniper
SWAT Secret Admirer

Visit the Author Profile page at Harlequin.com.

CAST OF CHARACTERS

Ava Callan—The K-9 handler is new to Jasper and trying to prove herself. Tracking down a bomber could be the key to her new start or the case that destroys her future.

Eli Thorne—The police captain and explosives expert is determined to protect his community from a bomber, but who will protect his heart from Ava?

Lacey—The German shepherd was supposed to be a drug-detection K-9, but when she alerts on bomb materials, she becomes the key to stopping a deadly threat in the small community.

Brady Nichols—The police lieutenant has a reputation for staying calm in any situation, and he'll need that steady focus when the investigation becomes increasingly complex.

Jason Wright—Being picked as part of the team tracking down the bomber is a huge opportunity for the rookie officer, but the case may be more dangerous than anyone anticipated.

Jennilyn Sanderson—The bartender has bomb training from the army and may be on an avenging mission. But no one knows what—or who—her next target might be.

Chapter One

She hadn't moved almost two thousand miles for *this*.

Ava Callan gritted her teeth as she climbed out of her modified patrol car and opened the door for her four-legged partner. Her gaze darted up, to the picturesque mountains in the distance, then back down, to the over-grown grass in front of her. Ahead was a line of con-cealing trees, and a little box house peeking through with its peeling paint and shuttered windows. The man who'd chosen to live on this big patch of land on the outskirts of Jasper, Idaho, wanted to be left alone by everyone. Especially the police.

Ava tapped her leg and Lacey, the two-year-old Ger-man shepherd she'd been paired with instead of a human partner, leaped to the ground.

Lacey's ears were perked, her nose in the air as she looked around, then up at Ava.

"Let's do this," Ava said, advancing slowly toward the house, her gaze on pivot as Lacey sniffed the ground.

Harold Bingsley, the man she'd been asked to do a wellness check on, had a history of methamphetamine use. Although Ava and Lacey had only recently fin-ished training together, Lacey had already started her training as a drug detection K-9 before Ava even left Chicago for this thousand-times smaller town.

This police call was routine and low-risk, but five years of working patrol and then narcotics in Chicago had taught her that no call was without the potential for danger. Letting her guard down was never an option. Not even here.

She'd parked on the street, mostly out of sight from the house, in case Harold was high, in case the sight of a police car gave him anxiety. According to his younger sister, who'd called from Oregon, he hadn't picked up his phone in a week. Maybe he was just angry with her for trying to convince him to move near family. *An endless argument*, she'd called it. But he didn't have any friends, and since he'd gotten clean, he had no one to visit. So, she didn't want to take the chance that he was hurt or sick and alone.

The slow trek along the dirt road toward the driveway was a far cry from Ava's last call out in Chicago. That had been a multi-agency raid on an illegal drug processing warehouse. She'd rushed in after SWAT had cleared it, enjoyed the congratulatory handshakes from a slew of federal agents on the work she'd done for the task force. Five months of her life had been dedicated to that bust. It had been her ticket to bigger and better things inside the Chicago PD. Instead of claiming them, she'd returned to the precinct and handed over her gun and badge.

There was a sudden tightness in the vicinity of her heart as she remembered her chief's frown, and the question he'd asked one more time. "Are you sure this is what you want?"

Shaking the memories loose, she focused on her surroundings. Beyond the couple of acres where Harold's house stood, the street was mostly commercial. Or at least, it had been at one time. Now, abandoned warehouses clogged the otherwise beautiful view, the exteriors slowly crumbling.

A beautiful May Saturday and Harold was presumably holed up inside instead of enjoying the cute little downtown. Not that there were a lot of entertainment options in Jasper, but he could have driven out to Salmon River, gone swimming or spread a picnic by the water now that it had finally started to warm up.

If she wasn't working, that's probably where Ava would have been. Pictures of the serene mountains and the river, so different from Chicago's constant hustle, had lured her here. That and the charming little downtown, framed by those towering mountains, had made her wire a security deposit for the house she'd rented, sight unseen.

She'd been determined to see the move as an adventure instead of a defeat. Three months later, that optimism was harder to come by, even if Jasper's natural beauty was better in person.

Skirting the rusted sedan and the motorcycle on its side on the long gravel driveway, Ava walked up to Harold's front door. She kept one hand near her holster as she watched Lacey.

The dog stopped beside her, staring up at her with intelligent brown eyes. But she didn't sit. Which meant that so far, she hadn't alerted on any drugs.

Nudging Lacey away from the door, Ava stood off

to the side as she keyed her radio and announced, "I've arrived at the Bingsley residence."

"Good luck," the cheerful voice of Jenny Dix, Jasper PD's only dispatch, came back.

Ava rolled her eyes. *Luck* would have been being sent to a real situation. Wellness checks ranked up there with parade duty. *Luck* would have been landing in a town where they appreciated her years of experience, where she actually fit in. Instead, she'd been given a K-9 and rookie duty. On the occasions when she tried to join the other officers after-hours at the local brewery, she'd always given up on feeling like part of something and gone home early.

Really, *luck* would have been not needing to leave Chicago in the first place. Her hand twitched toward the locket she wore under her uniform, with the photos of the family who had never supported her career choice. Family who was all lost to her now, for one reason or another.

Focus, Ava reminded herself. She'd made her choice. This was her fresh start and if she wanted it to work for her, she needed to work for it.

If that meant starting back at the beginning with everything—her career, her friendships, her sense of belonging—so be it.

Squaring her shoulders, she knocked on the door and infused her voice with friendly authority. "Mr. Bingsley? This is Officer Callan, Jasper Police. Your sister called us to make sure you were okay."

She listened carefully, ready to go for a weapon—lethal or otherwise—if he came out armed. He wasn't licensed to own a gun, but he'd been arrested with one in the past.

She heard nothing from inside, so she knocked again, a little louder this time. "Mr. Bingsley? I need to confirm you're okay or I'm going to come in to check on you."

Still nothing.

Holding in a sigh, and hoping she wasn't about to find forty-five-year-old Harold Bingsley dead, she positioned herself to kick in the door. A jolt of adrenaline hit, this simple forced entry the closest she'd come to the anticipation and anxiety of a drug raid since leaving Chicago.

The laugh stalled in her throat as the door ripped open and Harold lurched through it, his pale skin tinged gray and the pistol in his hand shaking violently.

Ava's gun was bracketed in her hands before she'd even consciously thought to reach for it. She slid in front of Lacey, who was trained to detect, not to attack and apprehend. Her heartbeat crescendoed, but she kept her voice steady and calm. "I'm here to help you. Put the gun down."

The gun in Harold's hand bounced rapidly up and down as he swiveled it toward her.

Her arms tensed, her finger tight against the trigger she didn't want to pull. "Harold, your sister thought you might be sick. That's it. You're not in trouble. Okay? Put the gun down."

His gaze darted around, not sticking on anything. His free hand reached up and started scratching at his face, leaving behind deep red gouges. The gun continued to bounce in his other hand, his finger inching closer to the trigger.

Ava held in a curse. He was definitely high. Which probably meant paranoid. It definitely meant dangerous.

She kept her voice calm and even, kept her feet planted solidly in front of Lacey, shielding her. "Harold, I need you to drop that gun before you hurt yourself, okay?"

His gaze skipped to the gun and he frowned, like he hadn't been aware he was holding it. He stared at it a long moment, his trigger finger jerking back and forth, almost nudging the trigger, then pulling away.

Ava locked her shoulders, kept her own trigger finger poised, ready to depress, wishing she was wearing a vest.

Harold yanked the gun up and Ava warned, "No!" as her finger started to tighten.

Then, he flung the gun aside into the long grass and darted away from the house, his gait uneven and clumsy.

Tucking her weapon into its holster, Ava ran after him. He was a good four inches taller than her 5'7", a solid fifty pounds heavier than her hundred and forty-ish. But he was also seventeen years older and in much worse shape. Plus, she had training and momentum on her side as she pushed off and tackled him, landing hard on his back.

Before he could recover, she yanked his hands behind his back and cuffed him, then patted him down for additional weapons as he muttered nonsense into the grass.

Keying her radio, Ava said, "I'm bringing Bingsley in. He pulled a weapon on me."

Jenny's response was lost under Ava's curse as Lacey went bounding past them, toward the abandoned warehouses.

"Lacey!"

The dog glanced back, barked once and kept going.

Yanking Harold to his feet, Ava pulled him along with her, following her K-9. Had Lacey scented on something? She hadn't at the house, but obviously Harold had had drugs to consume. Maybe he was keeping them in one of the abandoned buildings.

Ava picked up her pace to a slow jog as Harold stumbled along beside her and Lacey's lead increased.

At the entrance to the first warehouse—a massive building with cracked windows and some graffiti that reached a third of the way up the wall—Lacey sat. An alert that she'd found something.

Ava's heartbeat picked up again, anticipation at the slim possibility of getting a real case. Probably Lacey had just found Harold's extra stash. But maybe it was something bigger, a hiding spot for a distributor. "Good girl," she told the dog as she finally caught up.

Lacey glanced back at her, tail wagging, and Ava paused to pat her head.

This was the first time Lacey had alerted on something with Ava outside of practice, but unlike some K-9s who wanted treats or toys, Lacey's favored reward was a good ear scratch.

Checking her surroundings for any sign of people, any sign that this place wasn't actually abandoned, Ava keyed her radio again. Softly, she said, "Lacey alerted at the warehouse beside Bingsley's house. I'm going to check it out."

"Let me know if you need backup," Jenny's voice came back immediately.

"I'm good for now," Ava said, testing the door handle. It opened easily with a loud, high-pitched creak that made Ava cringe.

She spared a glance at Harold, who was using his shoulder to rub at his face where he'd scratched it earlier. "Is anyone in there?"

He just shrugged, but she wasn't sure if it was an answer or more scratching.

"Stay," she told Lacey as she peeked carefully inside.

Light streamed in through the damaged windows, illuminating layers of dust and abandoned machinery whose purpose Ava couldn't guess at. There were tracks in the dust in places, and a few abandoned beer bottles and other trash scattered on the floor, but the otherwise wide-open space looked clear and empty.

Easing the door open farther, Ava pushed Harold against the exterior wall and warned, "Don't move." Then she stepped slightly inside—not far enough that she couldn't chase after Harold if he took off, but enough to get a better look.

What she saw made her freeze, goose bumps rising across all of her exposed skin.

She backed out slowly, her hand already keying the radio, her breathing coming too fast.

Lacey hadn't alerted on drugs. She'd found a bomb.

Chapter Two

"Jasper PD just found a bomb. They need you on site now."

The Chief's words made Eli Thorne's pulse pick up. His hometown of McCall wasn't large. Even when tourists swelled it to more than double its population, he was more likely to get called to break up a bar fight than to defuse an explosive device. When he'd first gotten his certification from the FBI's Hazardous Devices School, his chief had thought he was wasting everyone's time.

That had changed quickly last year, during the packed tourist season, when someone had planted a bomb at Little Ski Hill and nearly destroyed one of their best winter attractions. Not to mention that there hadn't been enough time to evacuate everyone before Eli defused the bomb.

Eli stood at his desk, already planning the best route to get to Jasper, running through the steps he'd take when he arrived. "What do we know?"

"Not much. Just an address. Dispatch will get it to you when you're en route."

"On it!" He raced out to his police SUV, flipped on his lights and sirens and peeled out of the station.

Jasper, Idaho, was an hour north of McCall, but like most of the little towns peppering northern Idaho, they didn't have their own explosives expert. That meant Eli was on loan whenever someone uttered the word *explosive*.

Most of the time, the calls turned out to be false alarms; it was surprising the things people could mistake for a bomb. But if there was a real threat, an hour was a long time to wait. If the bomb was live, that time could mean the difference between life and death.

Eli punched down on the gas harder as he hooked around scenic Payette Lake, a lure for tourists and locals alike, and jumped onto US-95 North. He was ready for anything, with the back of his vehicle full of equipment he'd acquired slowly over the years after he'd gotten certified as an explosives expert. Equipment that had gotten a nice upgrade after his actions at the ski hill had helped him earn a promotion to captain.

At thirty-three, he was the youngest captain on the McCall police force. He wasn't stopping there. He loved his job, loved his community and planned to stay on the force until his knees or his back went to hell and he had to retire.

Hopefully, he had more than thirty years to go.

With a grin, Eli whipped around a guy in a Corvette who was ignoring the speed limit. The guy did a double take as he spotted Eli's police vehicle and slowed down.

As Eli got out in front of all the other vehicles, he pushed his SUV a little harder, making it to Jasper in forty-two minutes. There, he slowed way down, maneuvering carefully around cars and people strolling and enjoying the small downtown. He headed to the far side of town, one of the few places in Jasper where the buildings were eyesores instead of oozing with old-fashioned charm.

A pair of police cruisers blocked the road, but one of them backed up to let him through before he could lean out the window and ask. More cruisers blocked off the far end of the street, with nothing but a dilapidated house and clearly abandoned warehouses in between.

Eli parked as close to the warehouse as he dared. Most of the officers were keeping the perimeter clear, but one stood on the street across from the warehouse with a K-9 at her side.

She looked a few years younger than him with light brown skin, curly dark brown hair pulled into a high bun and a tight set to her mouth. The German shepherd beside her looked friendlier with a tail wag as soon as he hopped out of his vehicle.

"Eli Thorne?" the woman asked, her tone as serious as her expression with a little annoyance thrown in.

He was used to people being grateful when he arrived. Sparing her another quick glance, and wondering if it was him she had a problem with or just life, he hurried to the back of his vehicle and popped open the door. "That's me. What have you got?"

"I'm Officer Ava Callan," she said, peering into his open vehicle, curiosity on her face.

The dark tinted windows hid his expensive gear, allowing him to keep it ready to go at all times. As he pulled aside the tarp, there was an impressive array of equipment, including his bomb suit, tactical kit and his bomb-disposal robot with assorted attachments, controller and monitor.

"I had a prisoner with me when I spotted the device, so I didn't get close enough for a good look," Ava told him, her tone serious, her gaze skimming his equipment. "Lacey here alerted at the door."

The German shepherd wagged her tail at the mention of her name and Ava absently scratched the dog's ear.

"Technically, she's a drug-detection dog. Or at least that was my plan. More need than bomb detection. But she had some brief training with explosives before I started working with her. Good thing, too."

As she spoke, Eli carefully lifted his bomb-disposal robot and set it on the ground with a grunt. It was mid-size, meaning that when the arm and claw weren't extended, it just barely fit inside his SUV. It was also heavy at a hundred and fifty pounds. The cost had been donated to the department and if he dropped the thing, they wouldn't be able to afford a new one. But it was worth every penny; a sophisticated machine that rolled on twin tracks and could climb stairs, open doors and lift up to seventy-five pounds.

He left his bomb suit in the vehicle for now. It was heavy and awkward, and hopefully wouldn't be needed. More often than not, bomb calls were false alarms. Last week, he'd suited up only to discover a series of toilet paper tubes wrapped in duct tape and wires and topped with a watch at the McCall high school.

Whenever possible, the robot was better than the suit, anyway. It was a luxury he'd only come by recently and as he set it up, Ava stared.

"From the doorway, what was in that warehouse sure looks like a bomb," Ava continued, more of that same tempered annoyance in her tone.

Directed at him for not arriving faster or not giving her more of his attention? Or because of the other officers, all keeping their distance securing the scene, no one volunteering to stand guard at the warehouse with her? Knowing the department as well as he did, Eli didn't think it was because of fear. For whatever reason, Ava didn't fit in here.

"I didn't want to go near it. My background is in narcotics."

He shot her a surprised glance as he turned on the controller and started maneuvering the robot toward the warehouse. He knew most of the officers in Jasper, but he'd definitely never met one with a narcotics background. And with or without the attitude, he would have remembered her.

If she ever smiled, he had a feeling she'd be a heartbreaker. In this job, maybe that was why she didn't.

"I don't have experience with explosives," Ava finished, sounding slightly embarrassed by that fact.

"That's why I'm here," he assured her as he worked the controls, the movements like muscle memory now that he'd been using the robot for a few months.

The robot glided toward the warehouse at three miles an hour, pushing open the door farther and moving into the wide-open space as Eli watched the screen he had propped open in the back of his SUV.

Ava moved closer, looking at the readout as he tried not to notice she smelled faintly of cocoa butter. "This is some serious equipment for middle-of-nowhere Idaho."

"It gets better," Eli mumbled, most of his attention on the inside of the warehouse the robot's fiber-optic camera was showing him. The rusted machinery, litter scattered across the floor, newspapers and a dingy blanket that suggested someone had once squatted here only held his attention for a moment. Then, it was entirely focused on the series of galvanized pipes and wires wrapped together.

His pulse picked up as the robot got closer to the scarred wooden table where the pipe bomb rested, giving him a better look. End caps were fashioned onto either end of the pipes. A simple kitchen timer was hooked to the pipe bomb. Crude, but effective.

"You were right to call me," Eli told Ava.

"Is it live?"

"That's what we're about to find out." The kitchen timer didn't appear to be counting down, but that didn't mean the bomb wasn't set. It might just have meant it hadn't gone off when intended. The wrong movement now could still detonate it—assuming it was hooked together properly.

Thumbing the controls, he eased the robot around the table to get a better look at the back of the bomb. The lead didn't appear to be attached to the timer, which probably explained why it hadn't detonated. But it still could.

He eased the robot into position to take a live X-ray, a cool feature he'd been amazed that his department had been willing to shell out for. But they'd had help from a series of large donations after the attempted attack on Little Ski Hill.

Switching to his other screen, Eli stared at the image, studying it closely. Then the tension in his neck and shoulders released and he set down the controller.

"What?" Ava asked, on his heels as he strode toward the warehouse.

"It's not live. There's a lead, but there's no fuse in there."

"Then what's the point?"

Eli spun toward her and she stopped short, close enough that he could see the fullness of her makeup-free lips, the wary intelligence in her gaze.

She took a step back as Lacey strode up beside her.

"Did you see anyone take off out the back when you came over?"

"No. But given the layout here, if he timed it right, I probably wouldn't." She gestured to the thick line of trees behind the warehouse.

"Well, we've got two options. Either you interrupted him before he could open the end caps back up and fit in the fuse. Or he was experimenting with bomb-making and he's got another target entirely in mind."

Ava stared back at him, worry in her gaze.

Whatever the case, Eli had a feeling this wasn't going to be the last time he got called out to Jasper for a bomb.

Chapter Three

Already back in Jasper.

Typically, Sunday was Eli's day off. Today, he'd returned to Jasper, with an SUV full of supplies and a suitcase, after his chief had agreed to lend him out to their police force temporarily. With a potential bomber on the loose, Jasper needed more than just officers on overtime. They needed an expert on explosives.

Settled in the station's large meeting room with a cup of coffee and homemade apple strudel baked by Theresa Norwood, Jasper PD's longtime secretary, Eli glanced around. The room was filling up with officers. Some he'd known for years, who waved or called "hello," and a few he'd never met. But he found himself searching for a woman with a hard set to her jaw and a direct, challenging gaze.

Ava was abrasive, and overconfident for someone who couldn't have been part of the Jasper PD for more than six months. But there was intelligence in that direct gaze, and a story behind her go-it-alone attitude. If her background was in narcotics, it meant she'd come from a bigger city. Maybe she was running from a mistake on the job. Or perhaps she'd figured she could rise up faster in a town with lower crime, fewer officers. Either way, she didn't seem like a team player. He couldn't help being curious what had led her to this tiny mountainous town most people had never heard of.

Ava slipped into the room when it was mostly full, leaning against the back wall with Lacey at her side. Another K-9, this one a Labrador retriever, sat across the room with her handler, Lieutenant Brady Nichols. Jasper PD's Chief of Police, Doug Walters, was a huge proponent of Daniels Canine Academy, a police and search and rescue dog training facility located in Jasper. He'd brought on a number of K-9s over the years, had even had a K-9 partner himself before becoming chief.

Despite the other dog, despite the empty seats, Ava stood apart. From the lack of greetings, he suspected she hadn't yet found a way to fit in with anyone on Jasper's friendly police force.

As the Chief stepped up to the podium, Eli forced his gaze away from Ava. Doug was in his early sixties, and he'd been appointed as chief six years ago, but he'd been part of the community forever. Eli had worked with him several times before and found him to be blunt, but fair.

"Roll call is going to be a little different today," the Chief said as all the conversations in the room quieted. "We've got a couple of standard notes first. With the tourist season coming up, we're going to start seeing an uptick in larceny and petty theft, so keep an eye out. Last night, officers responded to a fight outside of Millard's Diner. One of the instigators wasn't a local, but we have a description of the man and his vehicle. Lieutenant Hoover will pass that around."

The Chief took a deep breath, his pale skin looking sallow under the fluorescent lights. "Now, on to why we have Captain Thorne visiting from McCall. As you've probably heard, Officer Callan and Lacey found a bomb yesterday. We got lucky and it wasn't live, but it did contain explosive compounds and forensics has confirmed that if it had been armed, it could have caused significant damage."

Over the murmurs from officers, he continued, "We have to assume whoever was building it has access to more materials and might try again. We're going to form a team to focus on this until we have a better sense of the threat. Let's find this guy before he can try anything else."

Officers around the room nodded, a few of them shooting Eli quick glances, probably hoping to get picked for his team. Chasing down a bomber was the kind of assignment that came along rarely, if ever, in a town like Jasper. Eli knew his team would be small, probably three dedicated officers. He already had some in mind who he could count on to follow his lead, who would work together seamlessly.

"Before we get to that team," the Chief continued, "I have a bit of bad news. Officer Callan did some digging last night into the ownership of the warehouse where the bomb was found. Most of you probably remember JPG Lumber, which went out of business three years ago?" As many of the officers nodded, the Chief said, "Officer Callan confirmed that the owners moved out of state. There's no obvious target here. Given that the door was unchained and someone had clearly been squatting there at one point, there's probably not a direct connection to the company. We'll still look into who worked there, see who might have comfort or familiarity to use it as a staging spot if this was just a practice run."

"What about prints? Or a lead from whoever was squatting?" Jason Wright, the department's rookie, called out.

He was young—only six years out of high school—but eager. Once a foster to the owner of Daniels Canine Academy, he'd come to the force with a desire to prove himself, to give back, that had resonated with Eli since the moment he'd met the man. As soon as the Chief gave Eli a chance to announce the team he wanted, he planned to include Jason on that list.

The Chief let out a brief laugh that sounded less than amused as he ran a hand through his thinning hair. "We have tons of prints, most of them pretty degraded. But on the bomb materials? Absolutely nothing."

A chill ran through Eli. The lack of prints suggested the bomber had worn gloves. That told him Ava had probably interrupted the bomber before he could insert the fuse and activate it.

A deserted warehouse far from anyone except a single recluse was a strange target, but maybe the intent hadn't been to harm anyone. At least not yet. Maybe the first goal had been to create fear.

The bomb might not have been viable when Eli arrived, but that was only because of the missing fuse. As Eli had dismantled the bomb, he'd seen the attention to detail the bomber had used. If he wanted, Eli was certain he could create a bigger, more deadly bomb.

Whether this had been simple practice or an interrupted bombing attempt, using gloves implied the bomber wasn't taking any chances. This wasn't a one-and-done bombing where the bomber didn't care if people knew his name—or maybe even wanted them to. This was someone with a long game in mind.

That made him even more dangerous.

"Captain Thorne and his team will work to identify the squatter, see if that was recent, see if he knows anything. Right now, we don't have any reason to suspect that the person who was squatting is the one who built the bomb. But Captain Thorne will take the lead in making that assessment. Then, he and his team will run down any other leads. We'll have three of our officers focusing on this as their primary objective. Let's stop this guy before he can do any real damage. Captain Thorne?"

Eli nodded and stepped up to the podium. He'd been right; he'd get three officers to help him. A good number, and he knew exactly who he wanted.

He kept his expression serious, but a familiar thrill was building inside. The opportunity to take on someone who meant this community harm and bring them down.

"Thank you, Chief Walters. Most of you know me, but for those who don't, I want to assure you—I may be a McCall PD captain, but my focus right now is fully on Jasper. We're all part of a bigger community and I'm glad to be able to help you stop this person. To that end, I'm happy to get the chance to work with a few of you on this."

He glanced at Brady Nichols, leaning back in his chair. The lieutenant with the olive-toned skin and close-cut beard had only come to Jasper two years earlier, but he and his tracking dog, Winnie, seemed like fixtures now. Eli had worked with him in the past and found him to be serious and focused. He was a bit of a hermit, but he still had the ability to project a calm confidence that put officers and civilians alike at ease.

"Lieutenant Nichols, I hope you'll be able to help out."

Brady nodded, sitting a little straighter in his chair as if he was already running through investigative avenues in his mind.

"We probably won't need Winnie on this, at least not to start."

The Labrador retriever dipped her nose and slid to the ground. Brady gave her a sympathetic smile and stroked her back.

"Don't worry. If we need to do any tracking, she's our girl."

The dog lifted her head again, tail thumping the ground.

Eli shifted his gaze toward Jason. The young Black man was sitting on the edge of his seat, tapping his fingers on the desk and looking hopeful. What he lacked in experience, he made up for with his tenacity.

"Officer Wright, I'd also like your help on the team."

As Jason flattened the smile that burst across his face, Eli glanced at the Chief, who nodded. The investigation would be good experience for the rookie.

Eli started to scan the room, looking for his final pick, when the Chief stepped closer.

"Officer Callan, we'd also like you and Lacey to be part of this team."

Eli felt a jolt of surprise. He tried to disguise it as his gaze darted from his team pick—Sergeant Dillon Diaz, full of charm and the needed ability to lighten the mood in the toughest times—to Ava. The new officer who couldn't seem to find a way to fit in, even in welcoming Jasper.

She was staring back at him, that same tightness to her jaw. This time, there was a mix of frustration and redemption in her gaze.

No doubt about it. She knew he hadn't planned to choose her. And she felt betrayed, probably since she'd been the one to locate the bomb in the first place.

He gave her a smile to show he was okay with the Chief's choice, even as his own frustration rose up. It was the Chief's territory, but it should have been his team to choose.

She didn't smile back, just stared at him as if he'd tossed her a challenge.

As the Chief dismissed the rest of the officers, Eli tried to rethink the strategy he'd had in mind for the team he'd assumed he'd get. Ava was a curveball he didn't need.

Not when there was a bomber on the loose, presumably anxious for another try.

Chapter Four

Eli Thorne didn't like her.

Ava ground her teeth as the idea rattled around in her mind. It shouldn't have mattered, not really. She wasn't here to be liked. She was here to do a job. But when you put your life on the line at work, forging strong bonds with people made a difference. What had come easily to her in Chicago felt like an uphill battle in Jasper.

The McCall police captain was an outsider, but even *he* seemed more at ease at the Jasper police station than she did. With his loose-limbed stride and easy grin, Eli had projected as much confidence inspecting the bomb as he had picking a team of officers to help.

She hadn't been on his list. Despite the fact that she'd found the bomb, despite the fact that she'd been the only one waiting outside the warehouse while everyone else stood at a distance.

He'd picked Jason Wright for his team, so obviously the white captain didn't have a problem with Black officers. Maybe it was because she was a woman? She'd faced that before—law enforcement was still predominantly male—but she hadn't gotten that vibe from him.

So, what was it?

From the back seat of her personal vehicle, Lacey whined.

Twisting her head slightly to glance at the sweet-tempered dog, Ava reached back and stroked her head. "What's wrong, Lacey?"

The dog leaned into the front seat, pressing her head against Ava's shoulder, and Ava couldn't help her smile. It was almost as if the dog sensed her frustration and was trying to make her feel better.

"Don't worry, Lacey. We're going to take a break this morning and have some fun."

Against her shoulder, Ava felt Lacey's body shaking, knew her tail was wagging.

They were headed to Daniels Canine Academy for some extra training, but for Lacey—and even for her—it was more fun than work.

Training K-9s was serious, but it was treated like a game for the dogs, to help them enjoy the work when it really mattered. Lacey definitely enjoyed it, wagging her tail whenever they went to DCA.

Ava felt a similar happiness there. Of all the places in Jasper, DCA was where she'd felt the most comfortable, where she actually felt like she might fit in.

DCA was on the north side of Jasper, across town from her little rental, and a fifteen-minute drive from the station, which was in between. It was Ava's day off, but it was a good excuse to stop by on her way home and see if any progress had been made on the case. Missing out on the start of the investigation, on top of being the cop who was forced onto the team by the Chief, felt like one more hurdle to overcome.

Her hands tightened on the wheel and Ava took deep breaths, trying to relax as Eli's bright blue eyes and contagious smile filled her mind. A smile he seemed to flash at everyone, except with her it felt tempered, forced.

"Let it go," Ava told herself as she drove underneath the large wooden sign with the silhouette of a German shepherd and the Daniels Canine Academy logo.

Still, Eli's easy smile, fading as the Chief announced he wanted Ava and Lacey on his team, then lifting again unconvincingly, didn't leave Ava's mind as she parked. Letting Lacey out of the car, Ava shaded her eyes from the early morning sun and stared out over the property. Behind her was the main house, but ahead the ranch was bustling. Emma Daniels's two rescue horses, a mellow brown American quarter horse and a more spirited black-and-white Appaloosa, were outside the barn, next to the kennel. On the outside agility course were a bloodhound and a Malinois training with their handlers.

As she headed toward the course, Emma strode over wearing jeans and a flannel, lifting a hand in greeting.

Ava couldn't help but smile.

The owner of Daniels Canine Academy was only a few years older than her, and was the person Ava had connected with most since coming to Jasper.

"Ava! Lacey!" As soon as she reached them, Emma bent down to pet Lacey, streaks of blond within her brown ponytail glinting in the sunlight. "Are you here for a refresher already?"

She grinned as she straightened again, and Ava

felt the tension easing from her shoulders at Emma's friendly demeanor.

"Sort of." Ava stuck her hands in the pockets of her jeans as she debated how much to share. Emma was close to the Chief, who'd taken her under his wing after her adopted father, a K-9 officer, had been killed on duty. But that didn't mean he would share police business with her.

Deciding to leave out what they'd found in the warehouse, Ava said, "I know Lacey had some explosives detection training before I started working with her. I figured the two of us could practice that a bit."

Emma's eyes narrowed slightly. "Any particular reason? Not that a dog can't specialize in several things, but I thought you'd decided drug detection was going to be your focus."

"She can do both already, though. It just seems like a waste not to keep her fresh on both skill sets."

Lacey looked from her to Emma, as if she, too, was evaluating whether Emma was buying the lie.

"I can't argue with that," Emma agreed, but she was still studying Ava with a little too much focus, as if she didn't quite believe that was all there was to it. "Let me get something set up for you. Piper has our new trainees under control on the agility course."

Ava glanced at the course, where the redheaded Piper Lambert, Emma's right hand at DCA, was demonstrating how to get a tail-wagging bloodhound to go through a tunnel to a tall Latinx man Ava didn't know. Probably someone in search and rescue, the other focus of the Academy.

As Emma headed toward the kennel, where she also kept supplies, Ava started at her name being called out.

She turned toward the house and saw Jason Wright ambling toward her, his hand linked with Tashya Pratt. The young Black vet tech stayed with Emma and also worked at DCA. Apparently, she was dating Jasper PD's rookie.

Ava forced a smile. She liked Tashya, who was a little shy but had a way with even the most skittish dogs. While Jason was friendly enough, he was trying to fit in at the station, too. Not something best accomplished by hanging out with the outsider from Chicago who hadn't even rated a human partner.

"What are you doing here?" Jason asked, pausing to pat Lacey.

"A little explosives detection training. What about you? You're off today, too?"

Jason shook his head. "Nah, I'm on in an hour." He tugged Tashya's hand upward, dropping a kiss on her knuckles. "Figured I'd talk Tashya into grabbing a bite before my shift."

"Hey, Ava." Tashya gave her a smile, then told Jason, "I'm just going to let Emma know." Then she jogged toward the kennel where Emma was emerging with a handful of supplies.

"You hear anything else about the investigation?" Ava asked, wondering if the McCall captain had kept the rookie more in the loop than her.

Jason shuffled his feet, but kept his gaze locked on hers. "Not yet. You?"

Ava shook her head. The confirmation that she wasn't

more out of the loop than anyone else was a small comfort, since the Chief hadn't approved her request to work on her day off. He'd warned her that an investigation like this, while time-sensitive, could also turn into a marathon. He didn't want her burning out at the start. While she could appreciate his logic, it still rankled.

"All set," Tashya called as she and Emma approached.

Jason nodded to her, then linked his hand with Tashya's and headed toward the drive.

"They're cute, aren't they?" Emma grinned. "I know they're adults now, but I fostered both of them and can't help feeling proud of how they're turning out."

Ava glanced back at the couple, surprised. She knew Emma fostered at-risk teens, but she was only seven years older than Jason. "Is it hard? Fostering?"

Emma gave a brief burst of laughter. "Hell, yes. Kind of like moving across the country to a town where you know no one and trying to find your place."

Ava must have looked surprised, because Emma gave her an understanding smile. "Don't worry. You'll get there. Now, give me a couple of minutes to set up and then let's put Lacey through the paces."

At the mention of her name, Lacey's tail wagged.

As Emma jogged toward the woods where she did some of the advanced training, Ava stroked Lacey's head. The motion was calming, easing the homesickness that had hit with surprising intensity.

Her colleagues at the Chicago PD hadn't wanted her to leave. Her friends had pushed her to stay, insisted that her brother just needed more time. That eventually he would forgive her.

But it had been five years since her parents died. Five years she'd spent reaching out to her brother, trying to make amends for something she never could have seen coming.

Blinking against the tears that rushed to her eyes, Ava took a fortifying breath. If Komi hadn't forgiven her by now, he never would. Since the only family she had left hated her, Chicago was her past.

She had to find a way to make Jasper her future.

Chapter Five

"Let's start with what we know," Eli said to his team, early Tuesday morning. Looking at Ava, who hadn't been on duty yesterday, he got her up to speed. "Yesterday, we dug deeper into JPG Lumber, the company that owned the warehouse."

Her lips tightened slightly, and she stood a little straighter.

Probably annoyed that he had retread ground she'd already tackled. But a cursory look at the status of the defunct company and the out-of-state owners wasn't the same as an in-depth check into grievances that might have outlived the company's demise, or easy access that could provide a starting point.

Right now, the only things they really knew about the bomber were that he could make a working bomb and he'd chosen to use the deserted warehouse. Since you could dig up a bomb recipe on the internet, the warehouse was their best lead.

"JPG Lumber, which manufactured lumber, was in business for seven years, but they were relatively small and just couldn't compete. According to the owners, who grew up around here, but moved to Oregon after their business failed, they never had any major problems with anyone. The bank took back the warehouse after the business failed, but like the other buildings on that street, there just hasn't been demand for them. It's been sitting empty since they left three years ago."

Ava's lips tightened even more, like she was holding something in, as Brady and Jason nodded from their respective chairs. But they'd both heard this yesterday.

"We've got a list of employees and we started going through them yesterday. Some left town when the company failed, but most are still here. No one pops as an obvious suspect, although we have a handful with something on their record, from domestic abuse to drug use to larceny. Today, I want to keep digging into that list and chat with the former owners of the other warehouses on that street, see if they have a different perspective. I also want to canvass the area, to see if we can figure out who was squatting, or if anyone else might have seen something."

"It's pretty deserted out there," Ava finally spoke up, her tone carefully modulated, but tension lay underneath.

"Yeah, it's a long shot," Eli agreed. "But right now, the only thing we know is that whoever made that bomb chose the warehouse. There has to be a reason."

"Could have been simple convenience," Brady spoke up, scratching his close-cut beard. "People who live here know it's empty. If someone wanted a practice location, it's a good choice. Unlikely anyone would notice, and with this kind of bomb inside a deserted warehouse, there probably wouldn't be any casualties." He shrugged. "Assuming this was practice for something bigger, which makes the most sense to me."

"I agree," Jason spoke up, his tone a little hesitant, but his gaze steady and sure. "Who does it really hurt to destroy a deserted warehouse? The bank? It's not even a local bank that owns it. Plus, it seems like they've cut their losses, since no one is actively trying to sell it."

"The target is odd," Eli agreed, "but the fact that this guy wore gloves still bothers me. If he's that cautious, why leave the bomb pieces at all? Unless we interrupted him in the process of setting the bomb to blow."

"Or he wanted someone to find it," Ava contributed. "Put the town on edge. Generate fear."

Eli tried to keep his skepticism off his face. "You and Lacey found it totally by accident. What were the chances someone else would have gone in there?"

"Maybe he planned to call it in anonymously, or figured eventually the unlocked door would get noticed. Or that whoever was squatting would be back," Ava defended her theory, one hand stroking Lacey's head.

The German shepherd was calm, her eyes at half-mast, belying her incredible detection skills.

"It's definitely possible," Eli agreed, mostly because he didn't want to sound like he was shooting down her ideas. Still, his gut told him there was another reason, because it had been three days since Ava and Lacey had found the bomb and the press hadn't gotten a hold of it. If the bomber wanted to sow fear, he could have left another bomb by now. No, this guy had a specific target in mind.

"Brady and Jason, how do you feel about tackling

more of the JPG Lumber employees today?" Eli suggested. "See if anyone harbors grudges, knows someone who does or knows of anyone using the empty warehouse for anything."

"Sounds good," Brady said, standing and stretching. He'd left Winnie at home today—apparently the Labrador retriever hadn't been too happy about it, but it made more sense to have a detection K-9 than a tracker right now.

"No problem," Jason agreed, the nerves in his eyes overridden by determination.

Eli glanced at Ava, whose own light brown eyes were filled with wariness. "How about you, me and Lacey do some canvassing?"

"Sure," she said, but he could tell she thought it was a waste of time, the kind of job handed off to a rookie.

Lacey looked more impressed, standing and spinning in a quick circle before staring up at him.

Eli laughed and gave her a pet. "Good girl." Then he looked at Ava. "Let's take my vehicle. I doubt we'll need it, but it can't hurt to have my detection gear with us."

She nodded silently.

He'd never had so much difficulty befriending a fellow officer before. Sure, there were officers he didn't like much, those he wouldn't hang out with outside of work. But on the job, he could usually get along with anyone.

Then again, he'd started off on the wrong foot with her by putting the Chief in a position where he'd needed to pick Ava for Eli's team. He wished he'd connected

with the Chief first, known the Chief wanted Ava and
Lacey on the team and announced it himself.

Holding in his frustration, and hoping he hadn't
made a mistake pairing with her today, Eli led Ava
and Lacey out to his SUV. As they hopped in, Eli asked,
"So, what brought you to Jasper?"

He pulled out of the station as he waited for her response. The extra beats it took for her to answer told
him he'd chosen the wrong topic.

"I wanted a change of scenery. I've always lived in
a big city, so I thought a small town would be nice. A
chance to relax, slow down a little."

It sounded like a practiced response, one that would
keep him from digging more. But he hadn't been a police officer this long without sensing a lie.

Instead of calling her on it, he tried opening up to
her. "I grew up in McCall—it's about an hour south of
Jasper—and came back here after school. I loved the
community, loved the way everyone knew each other
and looked out for each other. When I was younger, I
knew I wanted to be a police officer—my mom was on
the force until I was a teenager and she decided to move
into an administrative job. But I thought I'd want to join
a department somewhere bigger, more exciting."

He grinned, remembering his days at college in
Boise. He'd enjoyed having more options of things to
do, but he'd missed the feeling that everywhere he went,
he knew people. Missed the way people would smile
and wave at each other, the way they'd help each other
without needing to be asked. So, after finishing at the

police academy, he'd applied back in his hometown. He'd never regretted it.

"It's definitely different than Chicago," Ava said.

From the way she said it, she wasn't sure if that was a good thing.

He could imagine her in Chicago, walking the busy streets in her uniform, exuding confidence. Could even imagine her after hours, dressed casually the way she'd been when she'd stopped by the station yesterday, in jeans and a flowy green tank top, her curly hair loose and wild. In Chicago, she'd probably spent her evenings hanging out late at restaurants or bars with friends. Here, her options would be a lot more limited and most places were shut down by nine o'clock.

He snuck another glance at her, staring straight ahead as they reached the street where they'd found the bomb, and wondered if she'd last in Jasper. Or if she'd miss the faster pace of a big city, decide that whatever she was running from wasn't so bad.

Despite the fact that everything he said seemed to rub her the wrong way, he hoped she stuck around. Maybe it was just that he enjoyed a good challenge, but he wanted time to connect, to convince her that he was a good team leader. And to find out why she'd really come to Jasper.

Eli parked at the end of Bingsley's drive. Harold would be talking to a judge later today, both about pulling a weapon on a police officer and having that unregistered gun in the first place. For now, his house was empty.

"Shall we take a walk?" Eli asked, jumping out of the vehicle.

Ava was beside him quickly, with Lacey next to her.

"No leash?" Eli asked, surprised. As he spoke, he realized she hadn't been wearing one that day at the warehouse. She hadn't worn one in the station, either.

Ava stroked the dog's head and Lacey's tongue lolled out a bit as she leaned into Ava's hand. "She doesn't need one. Not for this. I have a couple, in case we get into a dangerous search area and I want to keep her close. But most of the time, I don't use them."

Eli nodded, impressed as he stared down at her dog. "I know none of the other warehouses are occupied, but let's just take a look. See if there's easy access to any of them or if anyone is hanging around. It's a long shot," Eli added at Ava's reluctant nod, "but—"

"It makes sense," she agreed.

Her tone still told him she didn't like being the one to do it. He wanted to argue with her—this wasn't Chicago. They were a small team and he hadn't asked her to tackle this part of the investigation because she was new or as some kind of punishment. She should have known that simply because he'd come with her.

He darted a glance at her as they circled the warehouse beside the one where the bomb had been found, Lacey sniffing the air as they went. Maybe that had been another strike against him, a sign to her that not only did he think she deserved rookie duty, but that he didn't even trust her to do that alone.

He cringed at the idea, but wasn't sure she'd like the truth much better. That he'd figured the chance to work together, just the two of them, would make her fall for his charms. Not in a romantic sense, but the way he could usually charm colleagues into seeing him as an ally.

Ava tugged on the back door of the warehouse, shaking her head. Her gaze shifted to a broken window twelve feet up. Her eyes narrowed. "It's an access point, and I've seen people scale some impressive things to get into a building. But usually the payoff would need to be something more than a deserted warehouse." She pointed at the uneven brick. "There are footholds big enough if you know what you're doing, but the glass is pretty jagged. Besides, even if someone went in that way, I think they would have still come out the door."

Eli nodded his agreement. People in small towns could get bored enough to do some outrageous things, but scaling the side of a building wasn't one that he'd encountered. Breaking a window closer to the ground to get in seemed more likely. "Let's check the next one."

As they walked, he noticed Ava's gaze on pivot, as though she were on a busy city street rather than between deserted warehouses and a beautiful forest. Birds chirped in the distance, and a hawk flew in a high lazy circle, but there was no sign of human life.

The trend continued as they walked the perimeter of the last warehouse on the street, which had once been owned by a company that made furniture. Along with the closed electronic manufacturing factory beside it, the company had moved to a bigger city. Most of the employees of both companies had gone with them, either commuting from Jasper every day or simply moving closer. Those moves had been a longer time ago, resulted in far fewer job losses than when JPG Lumber had closed.

Eli vaguely remembered that, because they had been a big employer in Jasper. When they'd closed their doors, quite a few families had left Jasper in search of other work. A few had stayed but faced foreclosures. From what Eli remembered, neighbors had pitched in and helped them stay afloat, the way small towns often pulled together in times of crisis. So far, his research hadn't uncovered anyone who hadn't been able to move forward from the job loss.

"I don't think we're going to find anything here," Ava said, hands on hips as she stood at the end of the street, past the last warehouse, staring at the mountains in the distance.

In between was nothing but more forest, and a winding dirt road that eventually led to farms. Maybe someone had walked this way to use the warehouses, but certainly no one was close enough to have seen unusual activity here.

Lacey, who had stayed by Ava's side the whole way but hadn't alerted on anything, lay down and put her head on her feet as if she, too, was discouraged.

Eli sighed as he stopped beside her, petting Lacey. "We'll have to find another tactic."

He tried to keep his frustration out of his voice. Police investigations were often this way—a lot of tedious hard work before one small thing blew open a case.

He hoped Ava didn't hear his worry, either. Because

whatever the bomber's goal, Eli was sure he wasn't finished.

They were on a ticking clock right now. They just didn't know the timeline.

Chapter Six

"I found the squatter," Brady announced as he set down his cell phone.

Ava's gaze jerked up from the paperwork she'd been staring at since returning from the warehouses with Eli. She glanced at Eli, whose bright blue eyes were intense, a hint of a grin on his lips as if he was looking forward to an interrogation—or the possibility that they'd just found their bomber.

"Who is it?" Jason jumped up from the far side of the conference table where he'd been working and hurried to Brady's computer.

Ava's head turned toward Brady, but her gaze still cut to Eli and that ghost of a smile. When she got a new lead on a case, she became serious and focused. She shouldn't have been surprised that Eli's reaction was excited anticipation. She'd known other cops like him, cops who enjoyed the job like it was a game.

She'd never quite understood it, though. She liked what she did, liked the satisfaction of putting criminals behind bars, the way it felt to help someone in need. But she didn't wake up itching for a good chase—even if she could appreciate the adrenaline rush of a takedown.

"His name is Ashton Newbury," Brady said, reading from notes he'd jotted on his laptop. "Twenty-five years old. Lives at one of the farms a couple of miles from the warehouse."

"I recognize that name," Ava said, trying to place it.

"He's on our list of employees who once worked for JPG Lumber. It was his first job. He started there when he was eighteen and was out of work at twenty-two when they closed down. Since then, he's had a few short-lived jobs at fast-food places, but that's it. He's been living at his parents' farm, but according to one of his friends, who also worked for JPG, he's been known to sleep out at the old warehouse when he and his parents fight. Apparently, they have a contentious relationship."

"Should one of us go talk to him?" Jason asked.

"Why don't we all go?" Eli suggested. "It's probably overkill, but we can't rule out the possibility that the person who was squatting also made the bomb. What else do we know about Ashton?"

Brady's dark brown eyes narrowed as he hunched over and typed into his laptop. A minute later, he shook his head. "Not a lot. He doesn't have a record."

Ava's fingers raced over her keyboard, performing her own search. She skimmed through the results quickly, wanting to contribute. "Social media is pretty minimal. He has aired some grievances about JPG and the way they *betrayed their employees*. Those are his words."

"Recent?" Eli asked.

"Last year. Looks like he was fired from a fast-food

job and was complaining about every place he'd worked. He seemed to hold the biggest grudge about JPG, probably because he worked there the longest."

"What about the parents?" Eli asked, looking at Jason.

The rookie darted back across the room, to his own laptop, and started typing.

Ten minutes later, as Ava was still scrolling through social media without finding anything else interesting, Jason said, "Parents have some history."

"What kind of history?" Eli asked.

"We've been out to their farm a handful of times, starting eleven years ago. Looks like the first time, Ashton called, saying his dad was threatening him. The next couple of times, the neighbor called. The farms are far apart, but each time, he was out working in his field and heard yelling."

"No arrests?" Ava asked, frowning.

"The incident reports say that when officers responded, everyone in the house claimed things were fine and promised to quiet down. No obvious signs of injuries, so nothing we could do. On that first call, Lieutenant Hoover—he was an officer back then—thought the kid, Ashton, who was fourteen at the time, was scared."

Eli nodded, his lips tight as lines appeared between his eyebrows. "So, we've got a kid who grew up with possible abuse, and hasn't been able to hold down a job since working at JPG. I haven't found anything that indicates he has explosives knowledge, but that doesn't really mean much these days. This kid grew up here. Does anyone know him?"

Ava shook her head, but Eli was looking from Brady to Jason, anyway.

"I've only lived here for two years," Brady said. "But I think I met the parents at a town event. I remember them being friendly enough, talking about their farm. I think they're known for their sweet corn."

"Yeah, that's probably them," Jason said. "Newbury Farms supplies vegetables to a lot of the restaurants here. Corn is their biggest crop. I'm familiar with the parents peripherally. They've got a big farm. Back in high school, kids used to go out into one of their back fields and drink."

The way he said it, Ava suspected he was one of those kids. "What about Ashton? He's close to your age, right?"

"He was in the class above me in school, but he used to skip all the time. I'd recognize him, but we never talked. It was a small school, but he was one of those kids who kept to himself. I do remember he was smart, though. Just didn't like school."

"Okay. Let's go talk to him," Eli said. "But let's tread carefully."

Brady stood and the rest of them followed him out the door.

Lacey trotted beside Ava, her steps high and excited, like she knew they were going to work.

Ava stroked her head as she hurried to keep up with Eli's long strides. He only had two inches on her five foot seven, but he moved like a runner.

She glanced at him from the corner of her eye, taking in that same hint of a smile. There was something compelling about his energy, something magnetic about the way his eyes widened when he grinned—which seemed to be often.

Maybe that was his trick for connecting with everyone so quickly. She'd try that, except a woman smiling at her colleagues a lot was often interpreted differently than a man doing it.

"Jason, why don't you and Brady take the lead, since Ashton might recognize you and feel more at ease?" Eli suggested as Ava tried to shake off her errant thoughts. "Ava and Lacey can check for any sign of explosives and I'll play backup."

The rookie nodded, a mix of nerves and excitement in his gaze as he glanced back at Eli.

"Your vehicle?" Brady called and Eli unlocked the doors with a loud *beep*.

Eli and Brady hopped into the front, while Ava and Lacey squeezed into the back with Jason. During the ride, Jason pet Lacey, his hand moving quickly at first and then more slowly as her presence visibly calmed his nerves.

Ava hid her smile as she gave Lacey a quick pat. Besides being a great detection dog, she was also a sweet, sensitive girl who seemed to pick up on people's moods quickly.

"I don't want to overwhelm them," Eli said as he drove, his gaze never leaving the road. "So, Ava, let's stay off to the side. Lacey can detect from there, right?"

"Depends. If the explosives are nearby, then yes. If

he's got them locked up in a basement or a barn or some-thing, probably not. But it also depends on the com-pounds. Some have a bigger scent cone than others."

Eli pulled up to the farm—a massive swath of land that looked bare without the five-foot corn plants Ava knew would cover it in a few months.

Ava scanned the field, catching a hint of movement toward the back field. They were parked before she could tell whether it was human or perhaps deer. "Might be someone out back," she let the team know.

"Keep an eye out," Eli said as they hopped out of the vehicle.

Brady and Jason strode up the long drive, directly to the front door. Ava and Lacey took the field to the left and Eli took the one to the right. Someone watch-ing out the windows would see them all, but if Ashton and his parents didn't know police were here until they knocked, the family would only see Brady and Jason. Hopefully that would make them more at ease.

Ava's gaze pivoted from Lacey to the door to the side of the house until they reached the front. Then she stood just a bit off to the side—not hiding, but not in direct line of sight from the door as Brady knocked.

After a minute wait, he was just lifting his fist to knock again when the door opened.

Then, everything seemed to happen at once.

Lacey moved toward the door quickly, sitting. An alert.

Goose bumps pricked the back of Ava's neck, and there was a blur of movement in her peripheral vision.

She pulled her weapon, spinning around just as a man she assumed was Ashton's father darted from the side of the house, aiming a shotgun at her.

Chapter Seven

What he'd hoped would be a quiet interview went to
hell fast.

His team reacted quickly, too. Eli hoped it would
be fast enough.

As Brady yanked out his weapon and spun to back
up Ava, Jason leveled his on Ashton, ordering him not
to move.

Lacey's head pivoted, but without an order from Ava,
she stayed planted where she'd alerted.

Eli, on the far side of the house, darted around the
corner, hoping the man with the shotgun hadn't seen
him. Or if he had, he'd be too focused on Ava and Brady
to realize why Eli was slipping around the back of the
house.

Had Mr. Newbury realized what Ashton had done,
suspected the police were here to arrest him and planned
to protect his only child? Did he think they were here for
some other reason, maybe for more fighting he assumed
had been overheard? Or was it something else entirely?

Eli had no way to know. But anyone who pulled a
shotgun on police without provocation beyond a knock
on their door was involved in something criminal.

They were also dangerous.

Pushing himself to move faster, Eli rounded the back of the house, scanning windows as he ran. Right now, no one knew where Mrs. Newbury was, or if she was also armed.

His heart thudded a little harder, imagining Ava facing a shotgun. He didn't know why she'd come to this tiny town from Chicago, whether there was an incident in her police record. Didn't know how she'd handle an armed civilian, whether she'd be quick on the trigger, too slow to react or good at talking someone down. He reminded himself that in the short time they'd worked together, she'd been professional and competent.

It didn't stop his anxiety.

Gun raised, Eli slowed at the back corner of the house, peering around it before moving slowly toward the front. Careful, silent steps as he approached.

Mr. Newbury was standing at the front corner, angled toward Ava. His finger was beneath the trigger guard and his arms were corded with tension.

The wrong movement and Newbury would see Eli in his peripheral vision too soon, might be spooked into firing.

Eli moved away from the house, farther from Newbury's line of sight.

Ava's voice reached him, calm and steady, infused with authority. "Mr. Newbury, we're here to talk. This doesn't solve anything. Put the gun down."

Eli could only see a sliver of Ava, her toned arm raised and bracketing her pistol, one long leg, her cheek and forehead. But he could picture her—all that smooth skin, the perfect cheekbones and serious eyes—lined up to a shotgun barrel. A twitch ran through him and he cursed his distraction. Seeing anyone in the line of fire was jarring, but he was too experienced to have it impact his ability to act.

Newbury shook his head, but his shotgun stayed steady.

Experienced shooter, Eli noted, a knot forming in his stomach.

A mix of anger and nerves rattled Newbury's deep voice. "Get off my property! You can't be sneaking around here."

"No one is sneaking around," Ava said, slow and easy. "We have a few questions for your son about his old workplace. That's it. You need to put the weapon down and let us do our jobs."

The shotgun lowered slightly, Newbury's biceps relaxing. "This is about Ashton's old work?" He sounded relieved, but also suspicious, like they were trying to trick him.

"Yes, sir. We need to ask him a few questions about something he might have seen. It shouldn't take too long."

There was a long pause, and Eli centered his weapon on the back of Newbury's head. His angle kept him out of Ava's line of fire and kept her out of his. If Newbury's finger moved against the trigger, the right head shot would prevent him from finishing that movement before he fell. It could save Ava's life.

Pressure built in his chest, an unfamiliar, heavier anxiety. McCall and Jasper were small towns, without high crime rates. He'd pulled his weapon before, even tackled someone who was holding a gun. But he'd never had to kill anyone on the job.

"Okay," Newbury said, lowering the shotgun to his side.

A breath left Eli in a whoosh and Newbury started to turn.

"Sir, I'm going to need you to put down the weapon," Ava said, drawing his attention back to her.

Eli could practically hear the man's scowl. But after another prolonged minute, he did it.

As Ava advised him what was going to happen, Brady rushed over and cuffed him, handing the shotgun to Ava. Sharing a relieved look with Eli, Brady walked him toward the vehicle as Eli settled his weapon back in his holster.

Ava did the same, looking a lot less rattled than he felt.

"Let's go talk to Ashton," she said, her tone serious and all business.

Eli followed her to the front of the house. He darted a glance at Brady, who gave a thumbs-up from beside the vehicle, where he was standing with Mr. Newbury.

Eli's SUV was set up to hold his bomb equipment, not to transport a prisoner, and he suddenly wished he'd thought to bring a second vehicle. But Newbury looked calm and somewhat chagrined as he nodded at whatever Brady was saying.

Ava and Eli stopped at a slight distance as Jason said to Ashton, "Can you step outside, please? We just have a few questions for you."

"What?" Ashton had his hands raised, his gaze darting from Eli and Ava to Jason to Brady and his father. His chin-length blond hair obscured his eyes and his jeans and T-shirt had a layer of dirt and dust on them. He chewed on his lip as he mumbled, "I didn't do anything."

Jason glanced at Eli as Ashton stepped outside, hands still up near his head.

Eli nodded back at him. He still wanted Jason to take the lead. Ashton was clearly nervous. Hopefully having someone he'd known as a peer talk to him would feel less threatening.

"Do you have any weapons on you?" Jason asked.

"No!" Ashton exclaimed as he lifted the bottom of his T-shirt to show his waistband, spinning in a slow circle. As he dropped the hem, he added under his breath, "I'm not my dad."

"Thanks, Ashton," Jason said. "Is your mom here?"

"No. She went to the store. Thank goodness," he added under his breath.

"Okay. We just have a couple of questions for you about JPG Lumber's old warehouse."

Ashton scowled, dragging his foot against the grass repeatedly. "This is about me sleeping there? Look, I've just got to get out of here sometimes. I can't afford my own place until I get a new job and I can't deal with flipping burgers all day. Who cares, anyway? No one has used it for years."

Jason glanced at Eli again, then over to Lacey, who was still sitting at attention.

"So, you just use it as a place to sleep?"

"Yeah. Look, the door has been unlocked for years. I never took anything, not like I could drag any of those machines out of there, anyway. And there's nothing else worth any money. Not that I would take it if there was."

"When were you there last?" Jason asked.

"Friday night," Ashton replied. "I came back Saturday morning and discovered my dad had a bonfire with my clothes. That's what I get for running out on an argument, he said." Ashton's frown deepened. "Asshole."

"Have you ever seen anyone else there?" Ava spoke up.

When Eli glanced at her, her expression was mildly curious, but the tension in her body gave her away.

"No." Ashton scowled again. "Why?"

"Do you have any experience with explosives?" Eli asked.

Ashton's gaze bounced to him, eyes widening. "No." He glanced from Eli to Jason. "What is this?"

"Are you sure you've never seen anyone else there, Ashton?" Jason asked. "Think carefully. This is important."

He shook his head. "Never. I wouldn't sleep there if someone else was using it as their getaway spot, too. I'd hit up a friend for the night."

"What about your dad?" Ava asked.

Ashton glanced at her, looking confused. "What about him?"

"Does he know where you go? Has he ever followed you there?"

"Hell, no. I don't tell him *or* my mom. With my luck, they'd drive over and yell at me some more."

Ava nodded, but her gaze was on Eli, not Ashton. She tipped her head to the side.

"Excuse us a minute," Eli said, following her cue and stepping out of earshot to speak with her. "What do you think?"

Her voice low, Ava replied, "I think he's telling the truth. I think Lacey alerted because of his clothes. From the look and smell of them, he's not lying about not having any other clothes. If he was last there on Saturday morning, it was probably before the bomber left the pipe bomb. But I bet the guy who made the bomb has been there more than once. I think Ashton has trace amounts of explosives on his clothes from being in proximity to where the guy was working."

Eli nodded. He'd been thinking the same thing. "Which means the warehouse *was* probably his practice spot and not a target. Maybe you were right about his plan. Maybe he'd seen Ashton there before—even if Ashton didn't see him—and he left that dead bomb intending for it to be found. But not by us. By someone who he figured would spread the word."

Ava nodded, looking troubled as she shifted the weight of the shotgun she still held. "I know it was my theory, and I stand by the idea of him trying to sow fear. But is the target the whole town? Does he want to make *everyone* afraid? Or do you think there's a deeper reason he picked the warehouse?"

"I wish I knew," Eli said. He glanced back at Ashton, who looked more afraid and confused than guilty. They'd have to watch him closely, in case he had them fooled. But in his gut, Eli knew he wasn't their bomber.

It had been three days since they'd found the bomb and they were no closer to figuring out who had left it. How much time did they have until he set another one? And would the next one be live?

Chapter Eight

There was no place like Idaho.

Eli took a deep breath of cool, clean air and felt the tension he'd been carrying since that morning's jaunt to the Newbury farm fade. It was getting late, and he'd come to town to grab some dinner after leaving the station. Rather than heading to Millard's Diner like he'd planned, he'd found himself in the park in the middle of downtown.

Instead of feeling like an anomaly of green space surrounded by buildings, the park seemed like an extension of the rest of Jasper. With the mountains in the distance and the big trees everywhere, it was the businesses and homes that seemed as though they'd been dropped into the wilderness. Along with Jasper's small old-fashioned downtown, Eli sometimes felt as though he'd been transported back a hundred years.

There was a chill in the air as the sun cast streaks of pink and purple across the sky. Still, families were out in abundance, enjoying the fresh air after a particularly bitter snowy winter. Although Eli enjoyed having a bit *more* in McCall—more restaurants, more events, more family and friends—he could see himself retiring to a place like Jasper. Could imagine himself spending the day at the Salmon River, swimming or fishing. Could imagine sitting out on a raised deck overlooking the woods at night, his wife beside him. He hadn't found her yet, but he knew she'd be like him—someone who loved the peace and community of a place like Jasper.

"Eli, hi!"

There was surprise and wariness in the voice and Eli recognized it before he turned around. He pictured her face, calm and professional even after confronting a man with a shotgun.

"Hi, Ava. You taking the evening to relax, too?"

Apparently after leaving the station, she'd gone home and changed into a pair of curve-hugging jeans, a flowy white top that emphasized her smooth complexion and a small gold locket that didn't quite seem to match her personality. Her hair was loose from its bun, the curls wild to her shoulders, some of them hanging over her eyes.

An unexpected kick of attraction hit him.

Beside her, Lacey wagged her tail and Eli bent to pet her, and to keep himself from staring too long at her owner.

"It's a pretty night," Ava said. "And I'm not much of a cook."

"I love to cook," Eli admitted. "But I haven't had a chance to do much grocery shopping since I got here. And the only thing stocked in the place I rented was ice. You want to grab some dinner?"

She looked a little hesitant, like she wasn't sure if he was asking her out or just being friendly to a colleague, so he quickly added, "We can chat about the case some more?"

The lines that had appeared between her eyebrows disappeared and she nodded. "Sure. We'll need to ask for a table outside since I've got Lacey."

At her name, the dog's tail wagged and Ava grinned at her, patting her head.

"How about Rose Café?" he asked. Millard's Diner had the best coffee in town and burgers he'd been thinking about since finishing his shift. It was also a cop hangout and for reasons he didn't want to examine too closely, he wanted the chance to get to know Ava better without interruption or curious eyes. The small restaurant away from the center of downtown was a little pricier, more of a date-night spot. But it also had good, hearty food and got enough family business to be a safe suggestion.

Ava looked surprised, then relieved. "Sure. They have some great outdoor tables."

Apparently, she didn't want to be interrupted, either. Or maybe she figured Rose Café would be more accommodating of Lacey. Or she just didn't want her coworkers to see her alone with him.

Eli glanced at her as they walked away from the center of downtown. Lacey strode at her side, no leash as usual.

He thought back to the little bit she'd told him about herself when he'd first met her outside the warehouse. Somehow, it seemed like it had been more than three days ago. "So, you specialized in narcotics back in Chicago?"

Her eyebrows lifted, like she was surprised he'd remembered. There was something wistful in her tone as she replied, "Yes. It was something I'd been interested in since I first joined the force. I had to put in my time on patrol first, but when a spot opened, I jumped at the chance to work narcotics. It was a great team. I'd actually just finished working on a big task force before I came here." Her words, which had gained speed and excitement as she started talking, slowed down toward the end.

"I grew up in McCall," Eli said, keeping his tone light and hoping she'd open up more about why she'd come to Jasper, maybe even give him the real reason for her move. "I went to school in a city, and even though I enjoyed it, I couldn't wait to get back to small-town living."

He smiled at her as they reached the restaurant and the hostess assured them it was fine to bring Lacey, then found them a table on the cozy terrace, next to a little fountain. The space was empty except for a couple and their two young children giggling and sharing dessert. The terrace was enclosed with a series of trellises, beginning to get overrun with green. In a month or so, flowers would fill them.

As Ava looked over the menu, Eli pretended to read his. He'd been here a handful of times and knew the menu well enough. Instead, he stared at her, trying to figure out the best way to connect with her. She was part of his team, whether he'd picked her or not.

Off duty, she looked more at ease, the tension in her

jaw gone, even her posture more relaxed. It made her look more approachable, too.

As she set down her menu, he picked up where he'd left off on their walk, still holding out hope that if he opened up about himself, she'd do the same. "My whole family lives in McCall, my parents and my two younger brothers. Even my grandparents, who are all in their upper eighties now, live nearby. All of my aunts and uncles and most of my cousins live within a three-hour radius, too. My parents grew up down the street from each other. They met when they were twelve and the rest was history."

A wistful smile tipped the corners of Ava's lips. "That's really nice. My parents moved to Chicago from the Dominican Republic when I was a baby. All of my extended family is still there. I haven't seen most of them in years."

Her smile faded and Eli wanted to scoot his chair around the table, pull her in for a hug. Instead, he asked, "What about your parents? And siblings. Do you have any?"

Lacey whined and Ava turned to reassure the dog, but Eli saw the stark pain in her gaze before she turned away.

"It's okay," Ava told Lacey, even though Eli knew the dog was responding to Ava's hurt.

"Do you know what you want?" the waitress asked, appearing at their table with a clueless smile.

Ava gave her order quickly and Eli followed, waiting until she left to say, "I'm sorry if that's a sensitive subject."

"It's fine." She gave him an unconvincing smile. "I'm just not close to my family anymore. My career got in the way."

"Oh." Eli tried to read more from her face, but her expression was closed off, her gaze averted. His own family had been incredibly supportive. Of course, he'd been following in his mom's footsteps, so it would have been tough for them to dissuade him.

There was an awkward silence, but before Eli could figure out a way to fill it, she said, "To be honest, it's been a challenge coming here. Not really because I don't know anyone—well, I guess that's part of it—but it's just so *different* from what I'm used to." The wistfulness was back in her tone. "In Chicago, even when you're alone, you're still surrounded by people, all of them going about their own lives. Here, it's like everyone knows each other except for me." She shrugged, not quite meeting his eyes. "I haven't fully adjusted yet."

She missed Chicago, missed the life she'd led there. Part of her still wanted to return. That much was easy to see.

He still had no idea why she'd really come here. He didn't know why she hadn't yet found a way to fit in either, but he wondered more and more if it was simply because she was guarded, used to having a shield up that people didn't know how to breach. Still, she'd picked a great community. He could picture Ava truly at home in Jasper.

She'd worked seamlessly with the team today. Even not knowing why she'd left a big force like the Chicago PD for what must have felt like a downgrade in Jasper, he'd feel comfortable going into a dangerous situation with her. From the way Brady and Jason had responded at that farm, they felt the same.

So, maybe the issue was purely social, that shield of hers making people think she didn't *want* to truly be a part of the community, that she was happier as a loner.

Eli had known many of the people in Jasper for years, but even if he hadn't, befriending people had always come easily to him. He could find ways to bring her into the fold more, show her that she'd chosen the right place to make her future.

"Anyway," she said as he realized he'd let the silence drag on too long. "About the case. I was thinking that there's not an obvious place to park near the warehouse. The shared lot between JPG's old building and the one beside it isn't in great shape and anyone parking on the street should have been noticeable to Bingsley. Maybe the bomber parked at more of a distance and walked, but then a quick getaway would be tough."

Eli nodded, even as his mind was still partly on finding ways to help her fit into the community. If he could do that, maybe she'd stay in Jasper.

His pulse picked up at the idea, at being able to spend more time with her. He genuinely liked her, he realized. Behind the shield she put up—maybe instinct from years of being a Black female cop in a big city—was a really interesting person. Someone he wanted to know better. Someone he could imagine in a role other than colleague. A true friend. Or possibly even more.

"Well, what do you think?" Ava asked as Eli tried

to wrap his mind around the idea that he was romantically interested in her.

When he didn't respond, she rushed on, "I checked before I left the station and Bingsley was released this evening. The judge gave him community service and he'll owe a fine for the unregistered gun. He was definitely high when I arrested him, but assuming he doesn't immediately get more drugs, I think he'd talk to me."

Eli nodded again. When she narrowed her eyes like she thought he wasn't really listening, he said, "Yeah, I think it's a good idea. Because I'm worried that we don't have many leads. It feels like we're just reacting, just waiting for the bomber's next move."

The words made his mind flip into work mode and he frowned. "We need to get in front of this, because whether the bomber meant for that inactivated bomb to be found or not, he probably knows we have it by now. If it was intended to scare the town, it didn't work."

Ava looked as worried as he felt. "Which means he'll probably try something more drastic next."

Chapter Nine

Ava zipped her hoodie up to her neck to ward against the early morning chill as she watched a couple of dogs in their runs beside the DCA kennel. She rubbed her hands together, trying to generate warmth and wishing she'd stopped for a cup of coffee on her way. But she only had an hour before her shift started and she wanted to get in as much explosives-detection training as possible with Lacey. If she and Eli were right, there would be another bomb somewhere in town soon.

Eli. The McCall captain had been so different last night than when she'd first met him outside the warehouse. Then, he'd been intensely focused on the task at hand, and she'd struggled to even talk shop with him. Yesterday, he'd been softer, easier to talk to.

"What are *you* thinking about?" There was amusement in Emma's voice, and when Ava spun around, it was on the woman's face, too. "Didn't you hear me calling your name?"

Embarrassment heated her. "No. Sorry. I guess my mind was wandering." Emma stared at her expectantly and Ava added, "Just thinking about how I don't quite fit in here."

It was partly true. Hearing Eli talk about how much he loved the area, how many friends and family surrounded him, she'd felt it even more acutely. She had no one.

Emma ducked her head as she pulled her hair up into a ponytail. "Jasper is a close-knit town. So many people have lived here their whole lives, going back generations. Everyone is friendly when you get to know them, but it can be tough when you're an outsider. Trust me, I know. I came here when I was eight, pulled out of a family that was…not good. But it was all I'd known."

Ava glanced around the ranch, surprised. She'd heard that Emma had inherited the ranch from her parents.

Emma smiled, apparently reading the direction of her thoughts. "Rick and Susan Daniels were my foster parents. Susan officially adopted me after Rick died, a few years before she followed." The smile faded, replaced by something bittersweet. "This place is their legacy."

"I'm so sorry." Her own loss was so much more recent and the words sat on her tongue, but Ava couldn't quite voice them.

"I still miss them, but I feel them with me when I train the dogs, when I foster like they did. Even with them gone, this place, the people here? They became my home. It wasn't always easy. I had times when I felt like I didn't belong at all. But when I was struggling the most, after my dad died, Chief Walters reached out to me, gave me the support I needed." She gave a self-conscious grin. "He kept me out of juvie, in fact."

Ava's surprise must have shown because Emma said, "It probably seems like I'm a fixture here, especially with all the work I do with your department. But it wasn't always that way. Everyone who comes here goes through that same transition, feeling like the one person in town who's missed some secret. It's just the way of small towns, when you're the one who doesn't know the people, doesn't know the history. It all happens, in time. You just need to let people in."

Emma stared at her, as if knowing there were things Ava wanted to say. Anxiety cramped her stomach, the words still not coming. Because she was afraid to let anyone in, afraid they'd still reject her? Or because saying them out loud would make them true, would make her own loss something she had to face instead of running away from?

A weight settled on her heart, a mix of anger and grief that she hadn't been able to shake in five long years.

Lacey let out a low whine and leaned into her leg, knocking Ava slightly off balance.

Emma put her hand on Ava's upper arm and squeezed. There was understanding in her gaze as she said, "The dogs are sensitive. They know when you're hurting."

Surprised, Ava looked at Lacey again, into the gentle brown eyes staring up at her. She'd never worked with a K-9 before, didn't have much experience with dogs in general. Stroking her head with a hand that trembled, Ava told her, "It's okay, Lacey. Everyone is okay."

"You do have friends in Idaho," Emma said, her tone soft and sincere.

"Thank you." Ava's voice sounded a little watery and she coughed, trying to get a handle on emotions she usually had locked tight.

She didn't know Emma well, but the DCA owner had always been friendly, even inviting her a few times to stay for dinner after training.

Ava had always declined, feeling too much like an outsider as Emma had traded jokes with Tashya and the three teenage boys who worked at the ranch. Now, she wished she'd taken Emma up on her offer.

Emma tipped her head, giving a broader smile. "Come on. I know I'm not the *only* person here you've impressed. Don't tell me Chief Walters isn't happy with the work you and Lacey are doing?"

A smile trembled on Ava's face. "I think he is." The smile stretched, thinking about her dinner with Eli. "And the team leader I've been working with on my new case seems to be getting over his initial dislike of me, which is a relief."

"Why didn't he like you?" Emma asked, her tone challenging, as if she didn't quite believe it.

Ava shrugged. "Maybe it wasn't dislike exactly, but he didn't want to work with me."

Emma waved a hand dismissively. "People stick with what's comfortable, that's all. Sometimes, you have to show them how to shake things up. Who's the team leader?"

"Captain Thorne. Eli. He's from McCall. You know him?" Ava found herself hoping Emma did, that she'd be able to share some insight.

Emma shook her head and Ava's shoulders slumped with disappointment.

Emma's eyes narrowed. Her voice was half teasing, half curious when she asked, "You're interested in this Captain Thorne, aren't you?"

Ava's face heated. "No." The denial came out too quickly, too forceful.

A brief laugh burst from Emma's lips, then she grinned. "If you say so."

"He's a coworker," Ava insisted. "I'm not even sure how well I like him." But as she said the words, she realized they weren't true. She hadn't liked him at first—or at least she'd been put off by the way he'd overlooked her for his team. Still, from the start, she'd been impressed by his skills in bomb detection and his confidence that bordered on arrogance. She'd envied his easy comradery with the other officers and wondered at his eagerness to head into potential danger.

They were nothing alike. Despite that, despite their rough start, something had changed last night, sitting on that terrace with him in the moonlight. She'd seen a glimpse of the man behind the uniform and she'd been more than intrigued. She'd been interested.

As she tried to process the realization, Emma waved a hand in front of her face. "All right, let's stop daydreaming and do some training."

Lacey gave a happy bark of agreement and Ava shoved back the mixture of bewilderment and nerves. She'd figure out what to do about her feelings later. Right now, it was time to get to work.

Chapter Ten

Eli didn't realize he'd been looking for Ava until she and Lacey jogged into the station's conference room.

They both looked energized, from Lacey's wagging tail and near-prancing steps to the upward tilt to Ava's head and the slight grin on her lips.

He felt a smile tug his in return. "Hey."

"Hi." She glanced around the room, probably expecting to see Jason and Brady there, but the other officers hadn't arrived yet.

She shuffled her feet, her smile becoming slightly self-conscious. "So, how long are you staying in Jasper?" Before he could answer, she rushed on, "I mean, is it a bad drive? Is that why you don't just commute? I've never been to McCall. I really haven't been anywhere in Idaho yet besides Jasper."

He studied her, trying to determine if it was his imagination or if something had changed since they'd sat together last night, gotten to know each other better. She seemed nervous, almost as if she'd felt the same spark he had at dinner.

He tried to hide a jolt of happiness. "It's an hour south of here. With a case like this, where I'm officially on loan to Jasper, I figured it made more sense to be here in case there was an issue when I was off duty. An hour is a long time if you've got an active bomb. McCall is great, though. You'd like it. It's a small resort town, survives on tourism just like Jasper, but it's bigger. Do you ski?"

"I've never tried it," Ava said, her gaze darting to the open doorway and then back to him. "But it looks like fun."

"We have some great skiing," Eli told her, hoping Brady and Jason took their time this morning and he got more time alone with Ava. They'd stayed until the restaurant had shut down last night, lingering over the dregs of their drinks long after they'd finished eating. He'd been surprised how natural it had felt to sit and talk to her after three days of awkwardness.

"I know Jasper has plenty of trails for hiking and they've got the Salmon River for kayaking, but you should try McCall's Payette Lake. There's also tons more shopping and dining, art festivals and live music. You should drive down when you have a free weekend. I'll show you around."

She nodded, dipping her head and stepping slightly away from him as Jason and Brady walked in, chatting about the log home Brady was building himself on a huge piece of property on the outskirts of Jasper.

Eli watched her from the corner of his eye, hoping he hadn't scared her off. He hadn't expected to feel an attraction last night, but now that he'd gotten to know her a little, he just wanted to know more. The best way to do that was to help her integrate into the community, show her around and let her see a real future for herself here.

"Sounds like the cabin is coming along," Eli said to Brady. To Ava he said, "Brady is building a house, all by himself."

Ava's eyebrows raised. "That's impressive."

Brady let out a brief laugh. "It'll be impressive if I ever get it finished. When I do, I'll invite you all over for a barbeque."

A hint of a smile pulled Ava's lips, and Eli felt one tug his in return. All she needed was a little help connecting and everyone would like her as much as he did.

"So, what's the plan today?" Jason asked.

They'd only formed the team three days ago, but already Eli could see it building Jason's confidence. The rookie was a solid officer, and Eli sensed that he had a great future.

Eli turned toward Ava. "Ava had some thoughts about Bingsley and what he might have seen."

Ava stood straighter and told them where she thought the bomber would have needed to park in order to be close to the warehouse.

Brady and Jason both nodded and Eli said, "Ava arrested him four days ago, so Bingsley might not feel so favorable about talking to her. Why don't you two go and talk to him?"

Ava's smile turned downward, the brief sense he'd felt from her of being a real part of the team fading. She hid it quickly, telling them, "Watch for paranoia. He was high when I went to his house. He was also armed."

Brady nodded, his expression serious. "We don't want a repeat of the other day with the Newburys."

"What do we think about them?" Jason asked. "I mean, I doubt Ashton was lying. Still, I don't think we can completely rule that family out."

"Agreed," Eli said. "We'll keep an eye on them. But I think it's more likely that Ashton saw something and doesn't know it than him actually being the bomber."

Ava nodded, and he realized he'd been watching for her input. Any concerns he'd had a few days ago about some negative police incident sending her to Jasper had faded, replaced by a solid respect for her ability to recognize possible threats.

"What angle are you two going to chase while we talk to Bingsley?" Brady asked.

Eli glanced at Ava, who looked as uncertain as he felt. They could search for more connections to the warehouse, but that list could be long. The chance that it was someone who had no connection at all was high enough that Eli wasn't sure he wanted to waste the time.

"Right now, the only thing I can think of besides Bingsley is the warehouse."

The others nodded, all of them looking as discouraged as he felt.

Unless Bingsley could give them a lead, the case was feeling stalled. And they needed to make more progress *now*, before the bomber struck again.

AVA GLANCED DISCREETLY at the time on her phone. It had been over an hour since Brady and Jason had left to talk to Bingsley and there was still no word.

She glanced across the conference table at Eli, expecting to find him staring at his laptop with his forehead furrowed and his lips pursed. Instead, he was staring back at her, something pensive in his bright blue eyes that made her pulse skip.

Had he been asking her out earlier, when he'd offered to show her around McCall if she went down there for a weekend? Or was that just the way small-town neighbors treated each other?

She was usually pretty good at reading people, but she had no idea. She'd grown up in the city, with parents who'd pushed her to succeed, supported her in her goals until the moment they hadn't. People on the force had been similar to her family's attitude: say it like it is, good or bad. No ambiguity. No uncertainty over where someone stood or their motives.

Or maybe that was just her perception. Maybe she'd assigned motives and never second-guessed herself. Even when she met a man she was interested in, she didn't waver. She made a decision—move forward or don't—and stuck with it.

With Eli, she wasn't sure what to do, how to act. If he was just being friendly, she didn't want to embarrass herself by acting like it was something more. If it wasn't in her head—if it really *was* something more—she didn't want to give him the wrong idea, either.

They were colleagues. That was all they'd ever be.

Just as she realized she'd been staring at him too long, lost in her own thoughts, he gave her an amused grin that lifted one side of his lips and made her heart pound a little harder.

"How's the search?" she asked, infusing her voice with as much professional distance as possible.

His smile turned quizzical, but he shook his head. "Nothing. There are about sixty people who worked for JPG at the time they dissolved who still live here. No one stands out as a potential suspect. Some are unemployed and a handful have some kind of record, but nothing screams bomber. Nothing that suggests a grudge big enough to want to blow up the warehouse."

She nodded, not surprised. "I didn't come up with anything, either. The list of people the owners gave you who were let go from the company within the year before they dissolved is pretty short. Two of them moved away from Jasper and the other three have full-time work and no sign on social media of bad will. But the company is defunct, the owners are gone. I don't think this is about JPG."

Eli ran a hand through his hair, making her notice threads of red in the short brown. "Yeah, I agree. I'm not sure where that leaves us with leads."

Ava glanced at her side, where Lacey lay on the floor. At her look, Lacey's head lifted and her tail thumped the ground.

Ava smiled at the dog, who read nonverbal cues better than any human she'd ever met. "What if Lacey and I go out and explore some other abandoned areas?" She turned back to Eli. "If the bomber's test run was interrupted, maybe he'll try again somewhere else. If he sticks to pattern, that means he'll probably return to the same abandoned spot more than once. We might get lucky."

Eli stood, stretching his arms up and tipping his head back.

He was only two inches taller than her, the dark Mc-Call uniform he wore each day despite working in Jasper emphasizing his pale skin and lean muscle.

He wasn't really her type. Not in looks or personality. But she couldn't stop staring, couldn't stop thinking about his words from earlier.

You should drive down when you have a free weekend. I'll show you around.

For the weekend. Not for the day, even though it was only an hour away. It sounded like an invitation to more than friendship, but Brady and Jason had walked in before she could figure out how to respond.

Not that she'd agree to such a thing, no matter how much she was starting to like him. Sure, he'd go back to McCall after the end of this case, but she got the impression that he worked with the Jasper police department—or at least coordinated with them—regularly. Not to mention that it was a small community, even several towns away.

She'd tried a workplace relationship once before. When things with DeVante had inevitably ended, it had been awkward even on Chicago's big force, despite not working the same shift and rarely seeing each other on the job. More than that, it had the potential to wreck the reputation she was trying to build here.

If she wanted to make Jasper her new home, she didn't want rumors going around about her relationships with anyone on the job, not even a captain from another force.

"Well?" Eli was staring at her as though he was waiting for an answer.

"Sorry," Ava said. "What did you say?"

He gave her another of those perplexed looks, like he was trying to figure her out, then said, "Are you ready? I'll go with you. If Lacey alerts, I'll have my equipment."

Closing her laptop, Ava pushed back her chair and motioned for Lacey to follow, trying to hide her nerves. She could have used some time alone, to get her emotions lined up with her head.

Because as she followed Eli out the door, awareness of him—of his loose-limbed stride and easy confidence, of the faint scent of some kind of woodsy aftershave—filled her senses.

Somehow, in the span of a few days, she'd gone from not being sure she even liked him to far too interested. Still, she wasn't going to let a fleeting attraction—because they were too different for it to be anything more—distract her from creating a new life for herself in Jasper.

Chapter Eleven

There weren't a lot of abandoned or empty buildings in Jasper.

The three warehouses on the street with Bingsley's house were an anomaly. Although the town wasn't big in terms of population, tourism kept increasing each year—not just in Jasper, but in the whole area—and businesses were paying attention. The latest addition was a river tour and rafting company that was having their grand opening soon. They'd grabbed the building practically before the old hardware store had put up their For Sale sign and moved off Main Street and into a more affordable space.

Eli was seeing similar growth in McCall. He was used to his town swelling to double or even triple the people during the summer and holidays, but Jasper had always been farther off the grid. He hoped neither of them grew too fast, lost the small-town charm and connectedness that had brought him back here.

"Not much is empty in downtown," Eli told Ava as he headed down Main Street, away from the Jasper police station. "The city is growing faster than space can keep up with demand."

She let out a small laugh and he remembered she was used to Chicago standards of growth.

He shrugged. "I mean that if a building in downtown opens up, it tends not to stay empty. The warehouses are different because most of the businesses here don't need that kind of space and it's not worth converting, especially since they're not near the main square."

"So, what have we got?" Ava asked, twisting in the passenger seat to face him.

He tossed her the notepad that he'd set on the seat between them, filled with the list of abandoned buildings he'd gotten from the Chief, who'd lived in Jasper all his life. Eli had known a few of them, places that had been empty since he was a kid. Others he wouldn't have found without someone who'd lived in Jasper a long time.

"None of these are even on the outskirts of the downtown." Ava sounded disappointed as she scanned the short list. "Seems less likely that our bomber would want something so out of the way if he's looking to create fear. Then again, he's probably nervous to return to where we found the first bomb. If there's nothing else around…"

"Like I said, the downtown is pretty small, but there's plenty of demand. Locals like the downtown, of course, but the draw is tourists. They come for the mountains and the river, hiking and rafting. Then they wander around the cute downtown for dinner or coffee. Or they come to Jasper as a day trip, for the homemade furniture. Those warehouses are mostly on the other side of town, and I doubt they'll ever go empty."

Ava nodded. "If I wasn't renting a place that was already furnished, that's the first stop I would have made after moving here."

"You're renting, huh?" There were plenty of rentals, mostly for tourist season, and since Ava had moved a few months ago, while demand was low, she'd probably gotten a good deal. But a rental was a lot less of a commitment than purchasing a home.

"I figured it made the most sense," she replied, not elaborating as she pulled up addresses from his list on her phone.

He glanced at her, trying to read on her face whether it made more sense because she wasn't sure she planned to stay, or just because she'd chosen a place over the internet. She was focused on the addresses, her lips pursed as she looked at the list that already had him discouraged.

Sure, a falling-down barn on twenty acres of land would be an easy place to sneak in and out of, and it was unlikely to have any casualties if the bomber wanted a practice run first. But it was also unlikely that a deactivated bomb would be found quickly and get people talking. And it was less likely to scare people in the same way that blowing one of the warehouses would have.

"Here's the first one," Eli said, parking on the gravel drive that led up to the barn. The land was vacant, the house long gone after an accidental fire had driven out the owners when Eli was a kid. Only the barn had survived. Faded red with a large hole in the roof, it was a known drinking and make-out spot for teenagers. Over the years, police had increased patrol here at night and cut down on all the activity. Now, it would be an easy spot for someone to leave a bomb with little fear of being seen.

Ava hopped out and Lacey followed, striding beside her owner as Ava took in the overgrown fields, which were high enough to block curious gazes from all directions. "It's kind of spooky."

Eli glanced around, seeing it as someone who was used to people, buildings and concrete everywhere might, as a place invisible to prying eyes, far from help. To him, it was serene, quiet except for birds chattering and deer bounding through the field in the distance.

"What does Lacey think?" Eli asked, keeping a close eye on the dog.

She didn't react to hearing her name, just moved forward with her nose in the air. Hyperfocused on the job.

"No alert yet," Ava replied as she scanned the fields and barn area as if they were in a densely populated city.

It was pretty unlikely anyone just happened to be hiding in the fields, but it couldn't be ruled out, and Eli listened closely for any sound out of place.

As they reached the barn door, which was standing wide open, Eli glanced at Lacey again.

The dog walked into the building at Ava's command, but showed no sign of having scented on anything.

Eli followed them in, squinting as he peered into darker corners, beyond the various panels that had once separated different animals. He stayed behind Ava and Lacey, letting them work.

The barn was dank, the scent of molding hay tickling his nostrils. Empty beer cans and a handful of cigarette butts were piled in one corner, but they didn't look recent. Above him, a pair of doves perched at the edge of the hole in the roof, singing their melancholy song.

"Anything?" he asked Ava as they reached the far end of the barn.

She shook her head, but he wasn't surprised. This was a long shot. If the goal was for someone to find the bomb and spread the news, it would have been left somewhere obvious that a pair of teens, focused on drinking or making out, would still have spotted it. If the goal was to blow up the barn, then why leave a bomb that wasn't ready and risk police finding it like they had at the warehouse? In that case, it would have been set off immediately.

Still, checking the deserted spots was the best lead they had, other than Bingsley. He glanced at his phone, hoping for news from Jason or Brady, but there was still nothing.

"Next spot?" she asked.

"Yep."

As he led her back toward the car, she said, "I might have to take Lacey back to DCA tonight, give her a chance to alert on something we set up for her to find, so she can get rewarded. I don't want her getting discouraged."

Eli glanced at her, smiling fondly as she pet the German shepherd.

"Maybe we'll get lucky." He tried to sound encouraging. Even though he didn't think they'd find anything, it had still been a good suggestion. It was also more fun than sitting at the station, digging through old records for the second time.

As they hit three more of the abandoned spots on the list—a dilapidated silo, a foreclosed home with the back wall missing and a massive old storage shed—it was hard to stay positive. All of them were empty, no signs of recent human visitors or bomb materials.

Ava and even Lacey were starting to look frustrated, too. Until his phone buzzed.

Eli glanced at it and saw Brady's name on the read-out. "5454," he told her as he handed her the phone. "That's the code. Want to see how they fared?"

She looked surprised that he'd so easily share the code for his phone, but she didn't say anything as she entered it and pulled up his text messages. Then her shoulders slumped and she shook her head. "According to Brady, Bingsley didn't seem high or evasive, and he claims he never saw any unexpected cars or people on the street. He also says he never went into any of the warehouses, that he had no reason to. Of course, that doesn't mean no one was there. It might just mean Bingsley has been too high lately to notice."

Eli swore, then gave her what he hoped was an encouraging smile. "It was still a good idea to check. So was investigating empty buildings around Jasper."

"I just wish it had worked," she said.

"We still have three more spots," Eli reminded her, pulling up to the next one, an old mill near the river. It had been turned into a coffee shop and then an ice-cream parlor before ultimately being shut down for safety issues with the structure. It had sat empty ever since.

As they stepped outside, Eli heard the distant laughter of people traveling along the river. Maybe a group canoeing or kayaking. The water was slow today, tranquil, with geese preening at the shore.

The parking lot, with its broken concrete and warped wooden picnic tables between it and the river, was empty. The old mill—Eli always thought of it that way, from seeing it functional as a young kid when his family would come out here for a change of pace—looked like it was closed up tight. There was grime on the windows and a board across the door. The wood waterwheel was partially moss-covered, but still felt like a landmark to him along the river.

Eli paused a minute, remembering the last time he'd come out here with his family a few months ago. His mom and dad had been laughing as they'd paddled a tandem kayak, his younger brothers egging each other on as they swerved into each other's paths. He'd been paddling more leisurely at the back of the group, taking in the sunshine and imagining a future with the family expanding; his brother had started talking about his plans to propose to his girlfriend that afternoon.

He'd pictured both of his younger brothers married, with kids, and himself, too. While both of his brothers were in serious, long-term relationships, he was still single. He wasn't in a rush to get married, but that day he'd felt a pang of anxiety, thinking that part of his life wasn't moving fast enough.

Walking here with Ava, he could suddenly picture her in a kayak alongside him, her curls loose and her head thrown back with laughter.

The image caught him by surprise. He faltered even as she picked up speed, moving toward the mill with Lacey.

He needed to focus on the job, keep things professional. He couldn't be distracted by this new attraction, couldn't let his desire to help her fit into the community shift into flirting the way it had earlier. Maybe once this case was over, he could ask her out. But not now. As the image of Ava beside him on the water, of Ava across from him on a real date flashed through his mind, he tried to ignore it.

His eyes narrowed on her, a different type of anxiety building as the daydream of some kind of future with her faded into the background.

Lacey was running toward the mill, Ava right behind her.

Eli glanced at his SUV, wondering if he needed to grab his equipment, then took off after them.

Just as he caught up, rounding the corner to the side of the mill and seeing a slightly open door, Lacey sat.

"She found something," Ava said, peering through the doorway. Then she glanced back at him, her expressive brown eyes wide and worried. "I think there's another bomb."

Chapter Twelve

"Don't go in," Eli shouted.

Even though Lacey hadn't made a move, Ava grabbed her collar as she glanced back at Eli with alarm. "Do you see some kind of trigger or trip wire? Would walking through the door activate it?"

"No. I don't know." He pushed down the panic he'd felt hearing her words about a bomb while she was standing on the threshold. There was no reason to think the bomber had rigged this one. But police had found the last bomb, so if he'd been counting on them searching other abandoned buildings, Eli couldn't rule it out.

"Let me get my gear and take a look first," Eli said, even as he stepped closer and peered around her.

The inside of the mill was set up like an old ice-cream parlor, with a long counter that wound its way through the store. Stools had once been pushed up all along the counter, in a rainbow of colors. Now, there was just the counter and the old freezer, with the door removed. On top of the counter was a pile of wires and fuses. Clearly bomb-making materials, but nothing had been assembled.

He frowned, scanning the space for anything else. "Did you see an assembled bomb or just the parts?"

Ava stepped up beside him, her shoulder brushing his, the scent of cocoa butter as calming as it was distracting. She pointed at the wires and fuses. "I guess not. I saw what's on the counter. Lacey alerted, so I assumed it was a bomb."

She turned toward him, her breath brushing against his chin, her lips with their exaggerated cupid's bow so close he could just sway and touch them.

"It's not?"

When he just stared, she backed up, bumping the door frame. "Eli, it's not a bomb?"

Focus. He swore at himself for getting distracted at a time like this. In the decade he'd been a police officer, no matter the distractions or emotions he'd faced, he'd never lost his focus before at a crime scene. How had Ava gotten under his skin so quickly, so deeply? It was exactly the reason he couldn't pursue her until this case was over.

"No. It's bomb materials, for sure. But it's not assembled."

He squinted into the space, holding his arm across the doorway as he searched for any sign that there were more materials somewhere, perhaps assembled. He couldn't rule it out. But he didn't see anything.

The bomber had obviously meant for this to be found. By a kayaker who stopped to explore? Someone who would call it in to the police, but maybe also tell all their friends or put a picture on social media? Or by the police, searching for the person who'd left it? If the plan was the latter, knowing that they hadn't shared it with the public before, what was the end game?

"Let's be careful," Eli said, his gut screaming that

something about this wasn't right. "You and Lacey stay outside, but call it in. I'm going to put on my bomb suit and get closer."

When he turned back toward her, Ava still had her hand locked around Lacey's collar, even though he doubted the dog would move without her handler's command. "You're worried that this seems like a setup?"

"Aren't you?"

"Yeah."

She glanced around, and Eli's gaze followed, to the towering trees and overgrown field behind the mill, to the river flowing alongside it. Sure, someone could pull their boat out of the river here and decide to explore. But it wasn't like the barn, known for trespassers.

Eli knelt closer to the door, examining the lock. It had definitely been forced, probably with a crowbar. Probably by the bomber.

"Call it in," he said again, striding back toward his SUV. He heard her and Lacey following, heard her on the phone with her chief as he stepped into his heavy, stifling bomb suit. With the helmet on, all of his senses felt dulled. Only his hands were free to let him work. Except for his hands, the suit would protect him from most blasts that a bomb like the one they'd seen at the warehouse could create.

"Be careful." Ava's voice trailed him as he waddled toward the mill with his nylon bag full of tools.

He glanced back at her, one hand across her forehead like a visor against the sun, worry in her gaze, and nodded. Then he trudged forward, mentally reviewing each step.

At the doorway, he bent down, searching for a trip wire, for any kind of triggering device. Seeing nothing, he took a fortifying breath and stepped inside.

He didn't realize how hard his heart had started pounding until he moved inside and the world around him didn't explode.

The inside of the mill was covered in a layer of dust, but not quite enough to make footprints obvious. Eli knelt close to the ground, the movement more awkward in his full-body suit. There were a few lines across the ground, as if someone had dragged their feet, but only near the bomb materials.

Sweeping his gaze down low, he looked for any sign of another device. Then he did the same thing at waist-height and standing. The only thing he spotted were the wires and fuses centered on the counter, like a pile of presents. A lighter was beside them.

Eli knelt next to the counter, eyeing the bottom of the pile for materials that were attached. An active bomb that might explode if he moved the wires and fuses on top. There was nothing.

Frowning, he stood and stepped behind the counter, then moved into the back room. It was tiny, just space for a sink, a few cupboards and an open spot where there must have once been a dishwasher. Slowly, he eased open the cupboards, but there was nothing inside except an old can of whipped cream on its side.

He made another pass of the entire inside to be sure, then keyed his radio. "As far as I can tell, it's clear, Ava. Can you bring Lacey in to do a better check?" He was good, but he couldn't see inside walls. A detection dog like Lacey would be able to smell a bomb hidden there. She'd also be able to tell the difference between chemicals on the bomb materials set out on the counter and a bomb somewhere else.

"On our way," Ava said. "So is backup."

She took longer than expected, but when she finally entered, she told him, "Lacey and I did a pass outside first." Turning to Lacey, she said, "Find the bomb, Lacey."

The dog's tail wagged as she followed Ava's lead. Instead of moving toward the materials, Ava walked Lacey in a pattern around the room, pointing for the dog to sniff in certain areas. When they reached the counter, Lacey sat beside the stack of bomb materials.

Ava rubbed her ears. "Good girl, Lacey. Good girl."

The German shepherd's tail thumped the ground, then Ava commanded, "Find the bomb, Lacey," and led her into the back room.

When they emerged, Ava shook her head. "Nothing else."

Eli nodded. He wanted to lift off his helmet, but it was too awkward to hold at the same time as his tools. And he wanted a closer look at what they'd found.

Bending his knees, he put himself at eye level with the bomb materials. There were a variety of fuses, multiple options to create a bomb that made tension knot Eli's back. Whoever was doing this had either spent a hell of a lot of time online researching or had real experience with bomb-making.

"Eli." The blend of excitement and urgency in Ava's voice made him turn toward her.

She was bending next to him, but her gaze was locked

on the shiny blue lighter beside the bombing materials. She pointed at it with a slightly shaky finger. "Is that..."

His breath caught as the light streaming in from the window hit it at just the right angle. "A fingerprint."

Their gazes caught and held.

"I think this case is about to break open," she said, excitement in her voice.

That meant very soon, he could ask her out.

Chapter Thirteen

As soon as they walked into the station, Lacey picked up on the frenzied excitement and started prancing around Ava.

Ava glanced around the open bullpen, searching for her team.

"Nice job, Callan," Sergeant Diaz said as he strode past.

She startled at the praise. "What happened?"

He paused, turning back toward her. "The print you found at the old mill had a match in the system."

Anticipation built in her chest and Ava picked up her pace, heading for the conference room. As she strode inside, Lacey pushed past her and sat at Eli's feet.

Eli laughed and gave the dog a pet on her head. Then his gaze locked on hers, excitement in his always-alert blue eyes. "We have a suspect."

"Who is it?"

Brady, who was seated at the head of the conference table, turned his laptop toward her. "Her name is Jennilyn Sanderson. She's got a history of violence, which is why we have her prints in the system."

Ava glanced around the room, from Eli to Brady and over to Jason, who was standing in the corner, his fingers tapping against his legs like he couldn't stay still. The anxiety transferred to her, a readiness to get Sanderson in a cell before she could detonate anything.

She wondered how long the rest of the team had been here before she'd arrived. She snuck a glance at the time on Brady's laptop, seeing that she was right on time. At the moment, it still felt late. "Are we getting a warrant for an arrest?"

"Not yet," Eli answered. "We need to proceed carefully."

"Why?"

From the way Brady and Jason both frowned slightly, they already knew the answer.

Frustration bubbled up, that somehow she'd missed so much this morning. It felt like a continuation of the problems she'd had since arriving a few months ago, always being the outsider.

Eli's eyes narrowed slightly, his lips pursing like he could tell what she was thinking. His gaze locked with hers and a spark of awareness shot through her. "This just came in. You didn't miss much. The evidence tech went over everything, all the wires and the fuses. The only item with any prints was the lighter."

"A good lawyer will get her cut loose, say the lighter isn't connected to the fuses or the wires," Brady said, even as he rolled his eyes. "Doesn't matter that it was *right beside* everything else, the only items in the place that didn't belong. To be sure we can make it stick, we need more. We don't want to spook her."

Ava nodded, trying to resist the urge to look at Eli again, to ignore the spark of attraction that just wouldn't go away. The pressure that should have decreased because they had a suspect ramped up instead. Things could get tricky when you didn't want to bring that suspect in right away. "She probably wore gloves when she left the wires and fuses—intending us to find them—but leaving the lighter was unintentional. Something that she was carrying but hadn't wiped down, because she didn't mean to drop it."

"Exactly," Eli said. "So, that's good luck and bad."

She nodded. Good because they had a name. Bad because it was too circumstantial. "We're still going to talk to her, right?"

"Definitely, but we need to dig into her history more first. You walked in about five minutes after we got the news on the prints, so we haven't done more than pull up her record."

Relief loosened her shoulders and Eli gave her a nod, like he knew why she'd been worried.

Tearing her gaze from his too-perceptive one, Ava peered at the image of Jennilyn Sanderson on Brady's laptop. In her mug shot, her lips were twisted upward into an angry snarl and her pale skin was flushed blotchy red. Her light brown shoulder-length hair was snarled, and her T-shirt was ripped along the arm, like she'd been in a fight. The expression in her light brown eyes said she'd won, but still wanted to go two more rounds.

"What was the arrest for?" Ava asked.

"Bar fight," Brady said. "Apparently it was a brawl, so multiple people were arrested that night. This was about five months ago. I wasn't on duty that night, but I remember hearing about it."

"I was there," Jason said, "but I wasn't inside. I was handling crowd control outside. The fight drew a pretty big crowd. It was around the holidays, so we had a lot of out-of-towners here for our winter festival. It's nothing like McCall's Winter Carnival—" he grinned at Eli "—but it's still a draw. That night, a lot of people had wandered into the bar after the festival."

"Bartwells?" she asked, surprised that a brawl would start at the cop hangout.

Jason shook his head. "No. Shaker Peak."

Shaker Peak was the spot for hard drinking and occasional dancing, whereas Bartwell Brewing was known more for their beers on tap and assortment of games, like pinball and dartboards. The cop hangout was clean and modern, whereas Shaker Peak was dark inside and looked like the kind of place that survived on day drinkers and out-of-towners looking to party.

"That makes sense," she said, remembering the one time she'd stepped inside, mistaking it for the "bar" that all the Jasper officers went to after work. She'd glanced around, seen only an old man in overalls with his head on the bar and a bored-looking bartender, and walked right out again. For days, she'd thought her colleagues had been playing a prank on her, until she realized she'd just misunderstood the location.

"Let's see what else we can learn about Sanderson," Eli said, settling into a seat, his gaze already locked on his laptop.

Lacey glanced from Ava to Eli, then followed him and laid down on his feet.

Eli laughed and paused to stroke her long fur. "You

do deserve a break, girl. You've done a great job help-ing us on this case."

Her head lifted briefly as she peered up at him, her tail thumping the ground, before she laid her head on his feet again.

The jealousy that streaked through Ava surprised her. Lacey usually followed her everywhere, whether they were on or off duty. Ava had even moved Lacey's dog bed into her bedroom, since the German shepherd had taken to sticking close at night, too. She and Lacey had bonded well since the Chief had paired them up last month.

Before that, Ava had mostly worked with whomever was available. She'd been paired with Brady on a few calls, and once with Jason. It was different here than Chicago, the smaller department meaning that officers often worked alone. When the Chief had brought her one of Emma's trained dogs to be her partner, she'd been offended.

It was a slight that was surely a result of her inability to fit in at Jasper PD. Still, since they'd worked together, she'd come to see the value in a K-9 partner. She'd con-nected with Lacey more than with any of the people in Jasper. Seeing the dog get attached to Eli so quickly made her wonder if she was wrong about her and Lacey's bond.

"I've got an incident report," Brady said, snapping Ava out of her thoughts.

She hurried to join the team at the table.

"What was the incident?" Eli asked.

Brady frowned at the laptop. "Guy called saying Jen-nilyn had smashed up his car. We responded, but by the time we got there, she was gone. We tracked her down, but soon after the guy changed his tune, saying it was an accident. According to the report, it clearly wasn't and we still did some follow-up. But ultimately, no arrest was made."

"Do we know why?" Ava asked.

Brady shook his head. "Dillon responded to the incident, so he probably knows more."

"When was this?" Eli asked.

"Four months ago."

"So, not long after the bar incident. Anything more recent?" Eli asked.

"No. Nothing prior to the bar fight, either, although I don't recognize her name. I don't think she's lived here that long." Brady looked over at Jason.

"I think she's a bartender at Shaker Peak. She looks vaguely familiar," Jason said. "But you're right. I don't think she's a longtime Jasper resident."

"Anything else in our system?" Eli asked, even as his own fingers continued to move frantically on his keyboard, his gaze moving rapidly on the screen as if he were speed-reading.

"Nope," Brady replied.

"What about social media?"

"Nothing obvious," Jason said. "But she could be using a shortened version of Jennilyn and not listing her hometown as Jasper, which means a lot more accounts to dig through. That could take a while."

Eli nodded, leaning back in his chair, his gaze moving to Brady. "Who was the arresting officer for Sanderson in the bar fight?"

"Captain Rutledge."

Eli's eyes rolled upward briefly, then he nodded. "Ava, why don't you, me and Lacey talk to Dillon Diaz and Arthur Rutledge, then pay Sanderson a visit?"

Brady's and Jason's gazes cut to her simultaneously. Even though she and Eli had paired up a lot during this case while Brady and Jason did the same, she read a mix of resentment and surprise there and dipped her head.

She wanted this chance, wanted the opportunity to prove herself. It made sense to have a detection dog when talking to Sanderson. Still, she was the newbie getting chosen to participate in the best part of the case. She didn't want her colleagues to think she was getting special treatment, to have one more reason not to fit in.

Her gaze met Eli's as she headed for the door, and she saw that same spark of interest she'd noticed the other night at dinner. She quickly averted her gaze, wishing she could eliminate her own interest as easily. Because if she didn't already have enough reasons to keep things professional, she'd just found one more.

Chapter Fourteen

"Captain Rutledge, can you help us out?" Eli called as he caught up to the man heading into the parking lot.

Arthur Rutledge sighed, glancing at his watch as he turned to face Eli and Ava. When he spotted Lacey, his lips twisted downward and he took a small step back, reminding Eli that the captain didn't like dogs.

Eli and Arthur were both five foot nine, but every time he talked to the captain, Eli swore the man tried to stretch taller.

Brushing his dark brown hair away from his eyes as a gust of wind lifted it, Arthur said, "What is it? I was just running out to grab a coffee."

"You might have heard that we have a possible suspect in the bombing."

Looking more interested, Arthur nodded. "Who is it?"

"Her name is Jennilyn Sanderson. You arrested her about five months ago during a bar fight at Shaker Peak."

Arthur, who was in his early fifties, but tried to look younger by growing his hair shaggy, pursed his lips for a long moment, then shook his head. "You're talking about that big bar fight? I arrested a lot of people that night. Name doesn't ring a bell."

"I think she was a bartender at Shaker Peak. Ava, can you pull up the arrest report?"

Before she could open her laptop, Arthur was nodding.

"Yeah, okay, I remember her. Former Army, so she knew how to fight." Arthur rubbed his knuckles, like he was remembering a tough arrest.

"Army?" Ava gave Eli a meaningful look and he nodded back.

They'd need to see if they could dig up details about her service, especially whether she had any experience dealing with bombs.

"Yeah." Arthur crossed his arms over his chest. "Several people mentioned it when I was asking about the fight. I think she liked everyone to know she's former military, because I remember she was wearing an Army T-shirt. She wasn't that big, maybe five-five, but she had some serious muscle. A lot of the people we arrested that night bailed out the next day, but not her. She went to court and ended up with community service. She put a guy in the hospital."

Surprised, Eli asked, "She only got community service?"

Arthur frowned, as if he didn't like it. "It would have been more, except enough people said the guy threw the first punch and she was defending herself. You ask me, she could have defended herself without breaking some guy's arm, but what do I know?" He shrugged, but rolled his eyes. "I'm not a judge."

"What else do you remember about the incident?" Ava asked.

Arthur stared at her a minute, his expression vaguely unfriendly, and Eli wondered if there was a story there. Not necessarily why Arthur didn't get along with Ava—it could have been anything from the fact that she had a K-9 to simply her being new and relatively unproven—but maybe it was contributing to Ava's defensiveness. After all, Rutledge was second-in-command at Jasper PD. He wondered if there was a tactful way to tell her not to take anything Arthur did to heart.

"Like I said, it was a big fight. Most everyone who was working that night got called over to help break it up. All told, we probably arrested a dozen people. There were plenty more who stood on the sidelines watching the brawl."

"What started the fight?" Ava persisted, her jaw tense.

Arthur snorted. "Some guys who drank too much and were making offensive comments to a couple of women on the dance floor. Harmless stupidity, but the women yelled back and then people were throwing punches."

Instead of arguing about what constituted harmless, Eli asked, "Do you remember anything else about Sanderson?"

His brows came down, then finally he said, "Besides her being aggressive and coming *this close* to resisting arrest? I think she might have been there with someone. I remember she was working, but I have this feeling someone had come in to see her that night. Maybe a boyfriend? I don't know if he was one of the people arrested or he just sat on the sidelines, watching his girlfriend beat someone up."

"Thanks." Eli sent Brady a quick text to look into a possible boyfriend for Sanderson.

As Ava thanked the captain and Eli started to head toward his SUV, Arthur called after him, "You want my take? I think Sanderson has a bad temper. She was quick to jump into the fray, even if it had nothing to do with her. I could see her deciding to set off a bomb somewhere. She seems like the type to take things too personal, and to take them too far."

Eli nodded as Arthur slid a pair of sunglasses from his pocket and put them on, then headed to his own vehicle. The captain had always rubbed Eli the wrong way, but second-in-charge at the Jasper PD wasn't a position he'd come by easily, even in a small town. That meant his opinion on a suspect was probably solid.

"Let's go pay her a visit," Eli said.

"What about talking to Diaz?" Ava asked as Eli realized she hadn't followed him toward the SUV. "He handled that incident where Sanderson smashed up a car."

Eli was anxious to get moving, but the more information they had, the better prepared they'd be for the conversation. Especially since they didn't want to bring her in to the station quite yet. "Yeah, let's find—oh, here we go." He pointed to the large glass front doors, where Dillon was exiting the station. "Hey, Dillion, you have a second?"

The Hispanic/Irish sergeant nodded, heading over to them in a few long-limbed strides. "What's up?"

Eli told him about their suspect. Before he'd finished reminding him about the incident with the smashed car, Dillon was already nodding, his dark eyes troubled.

"Yeah, I remember her. I didn't like that call at all."

"Why not?" Ava asked as Dillon leaned down to pet Lacey, who had stepped over to the sergeant and was staring up at him expectantly.

The German shepherd's tail thumped the ground a few times as Dillon paused to grin at her.

"Well, the guy who called to report his car being smashed up did it from work. He's in sales at one of the furniture stores at the edge of town. Can't remember which one. Anyway, he was working late one night, came outside and found his Beemer all smashed up. It looked like someone had taken a baseball bat to the headlights and the sides of the car. Everything except the windshield, which was intact but had the word *asshole* scratched into it, probably with a key. It was a mess. Not the kind of dents you can easily fix, either. Whoever did it put some real muscle behind the hits. They were trying to make that car virtually unsalvageable."

"Your investigation led to Sanderson?"

"Well, the guy—Kellerman was his name, Kurt Kellerman—led us to Sanderson. He gave us her name right away, said she'd been threatening him. He said he hadn't seen it happen, but there was no way it was anyone else."

"What was their disagreement about?" Ava asked.

"He claimed he didn't know why she disliked him," Dillon said, "but it was clear he was lying. I couldn't get him to budge on what motive she might have. So, I went to talk to her at that bar where she works, Shaker Peak. She claimed she hadn't done it, but gave me a bunch of hypotheticals. What if some guy sexually assaulted a friend of hers? What if that friend had seen the process of reporting sexual assault to police back in college and watched as someone *she* knew got no justice? What if she thought going to the police was a waste of time? Didn't the guy who'd hurt her friend deserve *some* kind of punishment?"

Ava scowled. "So, you think Sanderson busted up Kellerman's car as revenge for him sexually assaulting a friend of hers?"

"Yeah. I'm pretty sure it was someone who worked at that bar, too, because Sanderson kept her voice down while we talked, kept glancing around. At first, I thought she just didn't want anyone to overhear what she'd been accused of doing, but then I realized she was looking for someone specific. And I realized it wasn't so much her actions she was trying to keep quiet, but the little bit she was sharing about the assault. I tried to convince her to have her friend talk to us, but no dice. Without more to go on, there wasn't much I could do about investigating the assault. When it came to destroying the car, Sanderson was pretty good at keeping her words in hypotheticals. She never actually admitted to anything."

"So, then what?" Eli asked. "You couldn't find enough to prove Sanderson had smashed the car?"

"Not exactly. I'll be honest, I felt like I was digging into the wrong person. But we had a report, so I pursued it. But when I talked to Kellerman the next day to get some more details, he'd completely changed his tune. The first day, he'd been ranting and cussing Sanderson out, saying she'd been after him for months and finally seen her chance. When I went back, he had this really calm anger about him. He said he'd thought it over and decided he was wrong, that Sanderson had nothing to do with it. Said he didn't want to press charges against anyone and he'd just deal with his insurance."

"Any idea what caused his change of heart?" Eli asked, already suspecting the answer.

"I think Sanderson paid him a visit. I think she scared him. Hell, maybe he figured he'd gotten lucky, just having his car destroyed, and he didn't want to push his luck and have the friend press charges for sexual assault."

Eli nodded. "What's your take on Sanderson? Can you see her as a bomber?"

Dillon's lips twisted upward. "I don't know. I didn't get the impression that she would go for something indiscriminate like a bomb. But she was clearly discouraged by authorities in general. She mentioned being former Army, but she definitely had no love lost for anyone in authority. Maybe it was because of what her friend told her, maybe something else, but she seemed to resent not just my investigation, but also me."

Before Eli could say anything, Dillon continued, "I get it. Still, I think there was more going on there, because despite her obvious pride in being former military—she was wearing an Army hat when I interviewed her—she talked about military leadership in a similar way."

Ava looked at Eli. "Maybe Brady and Jason should try to dig into her military background? See if she left under questionable circumstances?"

Eli nodded, sending another text to Brady.

"So, do I think Sanderson could be the bomber?" Dillon repeated, and Eli looked up. "Yeah, given the right circumstances, I could see her being motivated by some kind of avenging mission."

Ava shared a worried look with Eli as he wondered what else Sanderson might want to avenge.

"The thing is," Dillon said, his tone ominous, "if it *is* her, she's good. That furniture store has plenty of security cameras, and she took just one of them out before she smashed up the car—the one that would have shown her on it."

"How'd she take it out?" Ava asked, her tone suggesting she had her suspicions.

"BB gun," Dillon said. "Perfect shot. Just one and the camera was toast."

As Ava nodded like she wasn't surprised, Dillon continued, "She's careful and she's not afraid to get her hands dirty. I honestly struggle to see her setting off a bomb where innocent people would get hurt, but maybe something has angered her and she thinks there are multiple people—or even a town—to blame. I can't imagine what it might be, but if it *is* her, you'd better get her behind bars fast."

Chapter Fifteen

"What's our play here?" Ava asked, glancing at Eli from the driver's seat of her police vehicle, a standard black Charger that was minimally modified for Lacey in the back. Even though it was silly, being in the driver's seat this time gave her a needed boost of confidence after their chat with Captain Rutledge had left her feeling sour.

Every time she engaged with him, she felt it all over again: she was the outsider and everyone knew it. It was never anything overt, just the way he'd look at her, eyes narrowed and lips tight, like he was staring at a suspect. The kind of thing she couldn't even really come out and ask about or he'd probably just call her crazy.

Right now, Ava tried to shake it off and focus on the case. They were headed to Jennilyn Sanderson's house to talk to her. It would be a tricky line to walk—getting information that might incriminate her, without tipping her off that she was a suspect. Or at least not tipping her off that she was a *primary* suspect, and potentially triggering her to act sooner than she might otherwise by placing a live bomb this time.

From what they'd heard about Jennilyn from Sergeant Diaz and Captain Rutledge, Ava worried that line was way too thin.

"I don't want to mention the lighter at all," Eli said. "If she knows we have forensics, I think it will spook her."

"Yeah, I agree. Maybe we can lead with the mill? Act like we're investigating some damage or graffiti and say someone saw her near there? Play it like we think she might have information about who *else* was around, and see if she gives us something useful?"

"What if we try that, but about the warehouse instead? Maybe in an attempt to give a plausible reason why she'd be there, she'll give us a hint about what her grudge is? It seems more likely that she has a direct connection to the warehouse than the mill. That could help us figure out her next potential target, get ahead of her."

Ava nodded, liking the idea of knowing what they were up against. If they could identify a motive, it could help them prevent a live bomb, but it could also help them get a warrant when the time came. "The thing I'm worried about for both approaches is what if these spots were just conveniently deserted? What if they were meant to sow fear, but the place itself doesn't actually matter? What if she's saving the real target for later, once the town is already afraid? Then are we just tipping our hand?"

"Yeah, I'm worried about that, too," Eli said. "But I'm not sure how else to go about this, because what Brady said about an arrest is spot-on." He sighed. "I'm anxious to talk to her, but maybe we need to spend more time digging into her background first."

Ava eased the vehicle off the road, onto the edge of a cornfield, and Lacey pushed her head through the seats, giving a slight whine.

Twisting to pet her, Ava said, "We're not there yet, Lacey. Hold on. You'll get to work soon."

Although Lacey barely moved, just opened her mouth and let her tongue hang out, Ava could have sworn the promise was making her smile.

Turning toward Eli, Ava said, "Maybe we should call Brady and Jason and brainstorm? The news about the print came in and we dove into everything so fast. Maybe we need a brief pause to strategize more. Plus, that will give us a chance to see if they've discovered anything else we can use."

He'd pulled his phone out of his pocket before she'd finished speaking. "Good idea." He called Brady and when the Lieutenant picked up, Eli put him on speaker and said, "Ava and I are close to Sanderson's house. We're hoping you've found something that will help us."

"Sorry," Brady answered, and Eli's shoulders slumped. "We haven't come up with the name of a boyfriend. We haven't found her on social media. And we don't have any information on why she left the Army. We've been searching, but the only thing we've discovered is that she bought her house in Jasper about six months ago. She hasn't been here long."

Eli nodded at Ava and she knew what he must have been thinking. That was something, at least. If she'd only lived here for six months, then either she'd come to Jasper with a preexisting grudge, or something had happened during that time. It definitely narrowed the search.

"We should focus on looking for any incidents since she moved here that could be triggering her," Ava suggested.

"Jason is already looking into that angle," Brady said. "Although based on what Eli texted earlier about Sanderson possibly thinking of herself as some kind of avenging force to help others, it might not be that easy to find what set her off."

"Worth a shot," Eli said.

"Oh, definitely," Brady agreed. "But I doubt we're going to have anything before you talk to Sanderson. Sorry."

"Well, that was only part of why we're calling," Eli said, giving her a rueful look. "We also want to strategize. I think I was a little hasty rushing out here without a plan."

Ava shook her head at him, not wanting him to think she'd been criticizing. She was more cautious by nature, but she admired the way he relied on his gut, the way he trusted himself. They needed to talk to Sanderson. Waiting too long could give her a chance to set up at her new target, and there was no guarantee they'd be in a better position to arrest her. One misstep could mean a literal explosion.

He gave her a quick grin in return, as if to say *we're good* and she felt the force of that smile all the way down to her toes. An unexpected flush heated her cheeks and chest.

His smile dropped off, replaced by a heat in his eyes as he held her stare.

She looked away first. She'd always been attracted to men who approached the world the same way she did, with caution and a long-term plan. Apparently, she wasn't just upending her entire life; she was also upending the way she evaluated others.

Maybe it was about time, after so long feeling guilty for who she was and the things she wanted, to give herself a little freedom. And maybe opposites really did attract.

Still, freedom didn't mean destroying the future she was building by pursuing another officer. Maybe it just meant not being too hard on herself for what she was feeling. A little fantasizing never hurt anyone. Because Eli Thorne might not be her normal type, but those bright blue eyes and that cocky grin were definitely fantasy-worthy.

She tried to keep the smile off her face, but she saw Eli's eyes narrow when she looked back at him, like he suspected what she was thinking.

Slowly, Brady's words penetrated, as if he were speaking way too quietly, and Ava tried to refocus.

"I think we should ask about the warehouse," he said as his words from earlier about Sanderson's avenging mission swirled in Ava's mind. "Ignore the mill entirely. The warehouse is the most likely place to be connected to motive."

"Yeah, we talked about saying someone saw her near the warehouse," Eli told Brady. "But if that was just an easy place to test a bomb…"

"We could end up with nothing," Brady agreed, even as excitement began to build in Ava's gut.

"What if we go about this another way entirely? We can still say someone saw her near the warehouse. If she gives us her connection to the place as a way to try to make it seem like she had a legitimate reason to be there, great. But what if we chat with her for a while, let her get comfortable and then level with her? Or at least, *pretend* to level with her?"

"What do you mean?" Eli asked.

"Well, maybe she'll claim she wasn't near there, or maybe she'll give up some other name, try and lead us in the wrong direction. Whatever she says, we can keep pushing her about who else she might have seen, or even if she saw evidence that someone else had been there. If we push in that direction long enough, hopefully she'll feel comfortable with the idea that we're not after *her.*"

Eli nodded slowly. "It makes sense. No matter what, she's going to know she's on our radar. It's a good idea to keep the pressure low. Make her feel like we want her help, so she doesn't feel pushed to act sooner."

"Right. Remember what happened when Sergeant Diaz talked to her about the car?" Ava reminded them.

"She gave up her motive without admitting to anything," Brady said, a hint of admiration in his tone.

"Exactly. We ask enough questions about someone else she might have seen, then we act like we're reluctantly telling her it's because we found bombing materials. See if we can get her to theorize about why someone might want to set off a bomb."

There was a long pause, but she could tell from the hint of a grin that pulled at Eli's lips that he was on board with her plan.

Pride filled her, the sense that she could really do this—she could find a way to fit in here, with her colleagues and in this town long-term. She might not be able to regain all the things she'd lost, but she could still make a future for herself where she was happy.

She was *so* ready to feel happy again, to shake loose the guilt that intellectually she knew was unfair. To stop replaying the disappointment in her parents' faces, the fury in her brother's eyes. To truly start fresh. To finally feel like she belonged somewhere.

"It's a great idea," Brady finally said into the silence.

"It could definitely work," Eli agreed. "We'll let you know how it goes," he told Brady. Then he stared at her. "You ready to do this?"

"Let's get our suspect to tell us her motive," Ava agreed, pulling back onto the empty stretch of highway.

They made it to Sanderson's house in fifteen minutes. The two-story home with wood siding and cheerful blue shutters was fairly small. It seemed even smaller because of its surroundings. The bartender lived on a big patch of land, with mountains visible in the distance and woods all around.

Ava felt a chill rush over her skin as she parked on the street and stepped out of her vehicle. The grass here was clipped short, not overgrown like it had been around the abandoned barn, but it gave Ava the same anxious feeling, like she was being watched.

Her gaze swept across the open front yard and she focused on the windows of the home, trying to spot anyone inside.

"You ready?" Eli asked, joining her on her side of the vehicle.

Pushing back her nerves, which were probably more a result of not being used to policing in the country than any actual threat, Ava nodded and opened the back door for Lacey.

"Let's do this." Eli moved like he always did, with confidence and certainty, heading toward the house without a backward glance.

Not reckless, but with an assuredness Ava rarely had without first prepping a plan and then a backup plan.

Ava's feet stayed planted longer than she'd intended and then she hurried to catch up, as Lacey trotted by her side.

She was about ten feet behind him when Lacey started barking, a deep timbre to her voice that startled Ava.

Eli glanced back at them, then whipped forward again. He pointed off to the side and mostly behind the house, where the hint of something man-made was visible among the trees. A shed, Ava realized.

Eli lifted his hands, making the motion of someone running, then took off in a run himself, toward that shed.

Had he seen Sanderson? Had she spotted them and made a run for it? If so, did that mean she thought they'd come to arrest her?

The jumbled thoughts raced through Ava's head as she tried to process what was happening. She squinted at the tree line as she started to run after Eli, but she didn't see anyone.

Lacey kept barking, more frantically now.

Had *she* spotted Sanderson? Lacey almost never

barked, especially on the job. She wasn't alerting, either, not sitting down to indicate she'd detected drugs or a bomb.

Dread hit Ava hard, slamming into her chest with the force of a suspect trying to knock her over. "Eli, *no*!" she screamed at him, even as Lacey overtook her, racing after Eli.

Her dog got out in front of Eli, barking at him and then running toward him, as if pushing him backward, as his confused gaze twisted toward Ava.

Then, the world around her exploded in a deafening blast of heat and fire.

Chapter Sixteen

The ringing in Ava's ears was overwhelming as she forced her eyes open, tried to get her bearings. Her lungs contracted painfully, refusing to give her enough breath, and the world spun. Hazy gray that passed to show sudden spots of blue, and little sparks dancing across all of it.

Ava tried to understand what she was seeing, tried to figure out what had happened. But her mind was as hazy as her surroundings. She blinked, bringing everything into sharper focus.

She was lying in the grass, on her back. Where there should have been sky above her was mostly gray smoke and small sudden sparks of fire, catching in the wind and then fluttering past.

A bomb has gone off.

The knowledge shot through her, tightening her lungs again, and Ava fought against the pain, pushing herself up on her elbows.

Where is Eli? Where is Lacey?

Panic hit next, a remembered fear that made her hands shake and tears rush to her eyes. *No, no, no. Not again.*

The fire that had engulfed her parents hadn't been

from a bomb, but a car crash. She hadn't seen it, but since the moment she'd heard of it, she'd been unable to stop imagining. That night, after she'd come home from a truncated Academy graduation, after she'd left the hospital being told they were gone before the ambulances even arrived, she'd seen the pictures on the news. A pileup, her parents in the middle of it. Her brother spared because he'd decided at the last minute to travel separately. In his mind, she was to blame.

Those flames, sinister orange and red shooting into the sky, still dominated her nightmares sometimes. Right now, they were directly in front of her.

The cute little house that had been standing moments ago was nothing more than stubborn blackened walls of brick and studs, fire consuming what was left in the middle. Pieces of the house, debris as small as the sparks lighting on the wind, and as large as a bent and battered claw-foot bathtub, were scattered around her. The scent of charred wood and plastic burned in her airways, made her eyes itch and tear.

What about Eli and Lacey?

Ava shoved to her feet, her balance as wavy as her vision. Or maybe it was the smoke and fire in the air creating the illusion that everything was still in motion.

Beyond a flaming piece of wall, thrown partially intact twenty feet from the home, were two figures, immobile in the grass.

"Nooooo!" The scream burst from her, terrified and anguished.

The force of it tore through her body, bent her in half. It left her gasping for breath, her tears blurring the rest of her vision, even as she stumbled awkwardly forward. A broken prayer repeated itself on her lips, a desperate hope that they were only knocked unconscious, that they were still alive.

She froze as Eli seemed to move, a twitch of his arm and then a partial roll.

Had she imagined it?

Squinting through the haze, she started moving again, faster now. It seemed to take forever to reach him, even though he hadn't been that far ahead of her. She dropped to the ground beside him as he groaned and rolled fully over.

A heavy breath of relief left her, and she swiped her arm across her face, trying to wipe away the moisture. She blinked at the sudden pain in her eyes, then noticed the layer of ashy soot on her arms, the smear of blood over her hand.

"Are you okay?" She could barely hear herself over her heartbeat pounding in her ears, the residual ringing making her want to shake her head hard.

"I'm okay," Eli assured her, even as she ran her gaze and her hands over him, searching for injuries.

He was covered in ash, too, lending a gray tone to his skin and flaking in his hair. There was a gash in the leg of his uniform and she ripped it farther, checking the skin beneath. The slash through his skin was ragged and oozed blood, but it was shallow.

He had other wounds, scratches across his forehead and blood and grass matted on his hands, probably from the force of his fall. But nothing looked too serious.

"I'm okay," he repeated, and she turned her hopeful gaze to Lacey, lying a few feet past him, closer to where the house had stood.

Her dog whimpered, her legs all twitching at once as she tried to roll to her feet. With another cry, she dropped back to the ground.

Ava shoved to her feet, spotting the blood, the short piece of wood piercing just above Lacey's hip. Tears rushed forward and she tried to blink them back, tried to be strong for her dog.

"Lacey, stay there, girl." She ran to the German shepherd, whose tail thumped once at her arrival. Her head lifted slightly, her pleading gaze locked on Ava's.

"Good girl, Lacey. Good girl." Ava heard the terrified waver in her voice as she stroked the dog gently, trying to see how bad the injury was.

The short blackened piece of wood—Ava had no idea what it was from—was embedded deep enough to have stained Lacey's fur and the ground partially red. It didn't seem deep enough to have hit an organ. But what did she know? Dogs were built differently than people.

She had some basic training in trauma response as a police officer, but she wasn't a vet. She didn't know whether to leave the wood in or to pull it out. She didn't know if Lacey would be okay.

"We need to get her to a vet," Eli said, suddenly beside them.

Ava nodded up at him, hoping he would have answers she lacked. When she'd trained to get a K-9 partner, she'd learned about basic care for Lacey in an emergency. But there'd been no guidance on what to do if a bomb exploded shrapnel into her.

"I'll carry her to the car and we can call it in on the drive," Eli said.

Ava continued to stroke Lacey's fur, the feel of blood on her hands making the tears well up again. "Should we be moving her?"

"We need to get her to a vet," Eli repeated. He glanced around, then ran for a flat piece of wood—maybe part of a long table—in the grass a few feet away. He reached for it, then lunged away, swearing. "It's too hot."

"The shed." Ava pointed at the shed he'd been running for when the bomb went off. It was a small green metal structure mostly hidden in the woods, but resting up against one side was a stack of wood boards in various sizes. It looked like pieces of a garden bed that someone had taken apart.

While Ava stayed with Lacey, whispering to the dog that she'd be okay, Eli raced for the shed. Somehow, after having just been unconscious, he looked steadier on his feet than she felt. His hand hovered near his holster and Ava remembered he'd thought he'd seen someone near the shed right before the explosion.

Ava's gaze swept the area, taking in the shed door, still closed. Empty? Or a convenient hiding place? Taking in the woods, dense enough for someone to be standing nearby, watching.

Had Jennilyn seen them coming? Had she rigged her own home to blow as a final exit after she'd set up more bombs somewhere in town? When they'd arrived, maybe it had changed her plans. Maybe she'd decided to slip out the back and blow it early, take them with it.

Was she still out there, potentially armed?

Ava's free hand darted to her holster as her gaze swept back and forth across the woods, looking for a color out of place, for any movement.

She saw nothing except Eli, his strides fast and sure. He grabbed the biggest board and then he was back at her side, giving her calm directions to lift Lacey with him.

The dog let out a small whimper when they lifted her onto the board, but she let them move her without any other complaint.

She and Eli strode to the car, holding either end of the board as they wove around debris that had blown out from the house.

They loaded Lacey into the back and Ava climbed in beside her, holding Lacey in place as Eli leaped into the driver's seat and put on the siren.

Then they were racing for the vet, and Ava's mind was on repeat, saying a prayer for Lacey.

Chapter Seventeen

The acrid scent of burnt materials—plastic and wood
and metal—seared the inside of his mouth and nose.
Even an hour later, it hadn't dissipated, just sent a new
reminder rattling his lungs with every breath.

Eli and Ava had been sitting in the vet's office for
forty-five minutes, waiting for word on Lacey. She'd
been rushed in for surgery while Eli had called in the
bomb to Jasper PD and told them about the figure he
thought he'd seen running for the shed. His imagination? Or Jennilyn, spooked enough to blow up her own
home if it meant taking him and Ava with it?

Whatever the case, this had been no pipe bomb. It
had been something much bigger, much more powerful.

During the multiple calls with Jasper officers, notifying them about what had happened and then fielding
follow-ups, he'd held Ava's hand.

She'd sat mutely beside him, staring at the wall, not
seeming to notice anything happening around her. In
shock.

Only now did she turn toward him, her gaze still
slightly unfocused, her voice hoarse as she said, "I
should go back. I should help at the scene."

He shifted toward her, taking in the smears of soot across her face and uniform, the grass and dirt streaking the sides of her arm and leg. There was more dirt smudged high on her cheek, the skin below abraded and slightly swollen. Deep scratches ran across the tops of both her hands, the blood dried and caked onto her skin.

Still, it was her eyes that worried him, that thousand-yard stare that said she was reliving the trauma over and over.

It had been her voice that had brought him back to consciousness, lying in the grass outside of Sanderson's house. The pain and panic he'd heard that made him fight to open his eyes and move.

"Your department has the scene covered. You don't need to worry about that right now." Eli squeezed her hand gently. "Lacey's going to be okay. Marie is a really good vet. She said she thought Lacey would make it through the surgery fine."

Ava's head jerked up and down, an imitation of a nod, like she was only partially hearing him.

"Ava." He took her other hand, tugged until she was twisting on the chair toward him.

She blinked a few times and finally seemed to focus on him. Then her pretty brown eyes welled over, tears spilling down her face.

Tugging a hand free, she wiped the tears away and ducked her head. "I'm sorry I'm losing it. I should be more professional. My job—"

"This is traumatic," he reassured her.

"She's just a dog," Ava said, her voice breaking at the end.

Eli stared at her a minute, surprised, then he asked softly, "You've never had a pet, have you?"

She shook her head, some of the curls that had been barely hanging onto her bun finally coming loose. They fell around the sides of her face and Eli tucked them behind her ears so he could see her expression.

Fear. Guilt. Embarrassment.

"Once you get to know an animal, you develop a special bond with them. If you've never had a pet, maybe you don't expect it. But they're all unique and special. They all have emotions and the capacity to love, just like us. You shouldn't feel guilty or embarrassed for loving her. She's a great dog."

Ava's forehead creased. "I don't feel guilty for that. I just—" She sighed. "Some K-9 handlers talk about their dogs like they're just a different type of law enforcement tool. That's what I expected when I started working with her. I didn't think…" She shook her head, then stared past him again.

"It's hard not to love them once you get to know them," he agreed. "I grew up with dogs and cats and a bunny, so I know how terrifying it is when an animal you love is hurt or sick."

Her gaze shifted back to his face, but he sensed she was only partially paying attention.

"You don't have pets now?"

"I do, actually. He's with my parents while I'm in Jasper. I didn't know what my hours would be like, but I have a Newfoundland. His name is Bear, because when I first brought him home, the little boys—three-year-old twins—who live next door yelled to their mom that I had gotten a pet bear."

Her eyebrows lifted. "A big dog."

He laughed. "Tell *him* that. He thinks he's a lapdog." His amusement settled and he squeezed her hand, making her glance at it. "He'd get along with Lacey."

As he said it, he realized he wanted to introduce them, wanted to see Ava and Lacey in his backyard, in his house. Wanted to get to know her better.

He'd felt it when they'd been at dinner together. Maybe before then, if he were being truly honest with himself. With every moment they spent together, that feeling was growing. The desire to see her outside of work, to get to know her more as not just an officer, but a person.

Her gaze rose from their hands and she seemed perplexed, like she hadn't realized he'd been holding her hand for the past hour. She gently tugged it free, then made a show of tucking her hair back into its bun.

"Ava?"

The soft voice made Ava leap out of her seat, and Eli followed her to where Marie Beaumont, Jasper's primary veterinarian, stood.

The vet had always struck him as cautiously friendly with everyone, but generous with her affection for animals.

Right now, Marie tucked her short brown hair behind one ear and put a hand on Ava's upper arm. "She came through the surgery just fine."

Ava's whole body seemed to relax, and Eli felt the same relief.

"Can I see her?" Ava asked.

"You can come back for a minute, but she's not awake yet. We're going to want to keep her under observation here for a few days, so we can closely watch her stitches because of the location. But I expect she'll make a full recovery."

Ava let out a heavy sigh, squeezing her eyes closed briefly. Then she whispered, "Thank you."

"It will be a few weeks before she can return to her normal activity and her K-9 duties, but she's strong. The wood was more shredded than I would have liked, but it didn't pierce any organs." The vet, a few inches shorter than Ava with a more compact build, gave Ava a gentle smile. "Come on. I'll show you."

Ava glanced back at him, a request in her gaze.

He didn't wait for her to ask, just said, "I'll come, too, if that's okay. Lacey saved my life."

A grateful smile lifted the corners of Ava's lips as Marie nodded and led them toward the back.

Before they reached the room where Lacey was recovering, a young Black woman who looked vaguely familiar hurried over and gave Ava a tight hug.

Ava looked surprised, then awkwardly hugged her back. "Tashya, I didn't know you were working today."

"Tashya helped out," Marie said, giving the younger woman an encouraging smile.

"Thank you," Ava breathed, hugging her a bit tighter before letting go and stepping into the recovery room behind Marie.

Ava made a slight sound of distress when she saw Lacey, bandaged and asleep on the table.

"She's doing great," Marie reassured her as Eli slipped his hand into Ava's again.

This time, Ava squeezed back, tightly.

"I know it looks scary, but I promise she's okay. She should wake up within the next hour. She'll be groggy for a bit after that, but before you know it, she'll be up for a real visit. It's just going to take some time." Marie put a hand on her arm again, stepping in Ava's path so she was forced to look at her. "Why don't you go home, get some rest? You can come back tomorrow and Lacey will be awake and starting to feel a little better. By the end of the week, trust me, you'll have a hard time limiting her running."

Ava nodded rapidly, like she was trying to believe it.

Eli tugged on her hand slightly. "Why don't we go and let Lacey rest?"

Her head swiveled toward him, her eyes wide. She nodded, but instead of moving toward the door, she stepped around Marie to Lacey. Carefully, barely making contact, she stroked the top of Lacey's head. Then she leaned close and, in a whisper she probably thought no one could hear, said, "I'm so sorry, Lacey. You'll be okay, girl. You'll be okay."

Then she backed slowly toward the door, not taking her gaze off the German shepherd until she was out of the room.

"I have to go see another patient," Marie said. "But I'll call you if anything changes. And you can call the office to check on her, okay? You know our hours, but I also live right upstairs, so I always peek in during the night to check on patients who are in recovery."

Ava smiled at the vet. She still looked shell-shocked, but there was gratitude all over her face. "Thank you."

"Go take care of yourself now." Marie looked at him and said, "Make sure she does, okay?"

"Yes, ma'am," Eli told the woman, who was only a few years older than him.

Then he led Ava outside and opened the passenger door for her. She looked briefly surprised; it was her car. Luckily, she'd parked on the street at Jennilyn's place, so it hadn't been damaged, except for a big dent in the hood from a nearly intact toaster oven that had been catapulted in the blast.

When he climbed into the driver's seat, Eli felt the adrenaline that had been carrying him since he'd woken up on the grass, his ears ringing and his body aching, fade in a sudden rush. It left him so exhausted that he wondered if he should drive. But Ava was in no shape to do it, so he took a couple of deep breaths until he felt a little better. Then he started the engine and asked, "What's your address?"

She sat a little straighter, making a valiant effort to appear normal. It didn't reach her eyes, which were still wide with shock. "Shouldn't we go to the station? I'm sure there are things to do. I want to see how everything is going at Sanderson's house and—"

"Brady and Jason will keep updating us," Eli said. "They've been texting while we were at the vet's. So far, we don't know a lot, other than no one was spotted by the shed or in the woods. The shed was locked. We don't know yet if there were any casualties in the house."

"Don't you think—"

"We're no good to anyone right now," Eli insisted. "I'm exhausted. You're exhausted. We need to get cleaned up, get some rest and come back fresh tomorrow. There will still be plenty to do. If Sanderson is in the wind, hopefully it will slow her down with whatever her ultimate target is."

There was a long pause and he was readying his next argument when she sighed and gave him an address.

Thankfully, she didn't live too far from Marie's vet office downtown. Still, by the time he'd reached the short drive in front of her rental, a cute two-story with a wraparound porch and a great view of the mountains, he wasn't sure he could have driven much farther.

He'd been through stressful calls before, but he hadn't felt this level of exhaustion since he'd defused that bomb at Little Ski Hill.

He turned off the engine and glanced at Ava, who had stared mutely through the windshield the entire drive. "I don't think I can make it back. Can I come in?"

Surprise flashed across her face, followed by uncertainty. Before he could say he'd get a ride, she nodded. Her voice barely above a whisper, she said, "I'd like that."

Chapter Eighteen

She'd lived in Jasper for months and this was the first time she'd invited anyone inside her house.

Ava glanced at Eli from the corner of her eyes, watching him take in the open-concept space. The front hall flowed right into the kitchen, which flowed right into a great room with expansive windows. And that view of the mountains, the one that had made her sign a rental agreement from across the country.

A dream of a new life wrapped up in a simple, serene view. She'd held tight to it ever since, but with each day she tried and failed to fit in, the dream had seemed further away.

Trying not to think about all the things that seemed out of reach right now, she followed Eli into the great room. The furnishings had come with the rental, a mix of raw-edge wood she loved and plaid she could have done without. She hadn't added any of her own touches yet, had put most of her belongings in storage back in Chicago.

At the time, she'd called it convenience. Why did she need to pay to bring her furniture across the country when the house already had plenty? She'd intended to have them brought over once she moved out of a rental and into a home she bought. But she'd been here for several months now and hadn't even considered looking at homes for sale. Suddenly she wondered if it had been her way of not fully committing.

As much as she wanted this fresh start, she'd left a part of herself in Chicago. The part that still hoped there was a chance to mend things with her brother. The part that wished she could go back in time and not pressure her parents to come to her Academy graduation. If she hadn't pushed, maybe they'd still be alive.

The idea pinched her heart, an ache that was never far from her thoughts.

"What a gorgeous view."

It took a minute for Eli's words to penetrate, and Ava tried to smile. It felt forced and shaky and she gave up on it. Instead, she nodded and said, "It's why I chose this place."

"The house? Or Jasper?"

"Both."

He nodded, staring at her as if that answer told him a lot, but that he still wanted to know more.

The idea made her shiver. She wanted friends, wanted to forge bonds here that would take Jasper from the place she lived to truly being her home. But reaching out hadn't been easy.

In Chicago, she'd been more fearless about making friends. She was cautious at work, of course, especially after that failed relationship with DeVante. It had put a strain on colleagues' faces that always made her wonder, what had they heard?

Still, it was much more than just her relationship with DeVante souring too publicly. It was the years of trying to rebuild one of the most important relationships in her life—with her brother—and ultimately failing. No matter what spin she tried to put on it, coming to Jasper was her admitting that failure.

"Why did you come here, Ava?"

Eli's words were soft, empathetic, like he already knew the answer held some kind of tragedy.

When she focused on him, she realized he was no longer standing at her big window, but right beside her. The scent of his woodsy aftershave blended with the scent of smoke that she didn't think even a dozen washes could take out of her uniform or her hair.

His nearness made her pulse pick up, made her breathing shallow. It seemed like the more she tried to ignore this attraction, the more it grew. It wasn't just physical desire. She wanted to be honest with him, wanted him to really know her. And she wanted to know him in return.

She took a deep breath, her nose itching at the smoke. All connections, whether they were friendships or something more, took a leap of faith. Maybe it was time to leap again.

She pulled the locket out from underneath her uniform, happy to see it hadn't been damaged when the blast had thrown her to the ground. Opening it with hands that shook, she held it slightly away from her body to show Eli.

He leaned in, that woodsy scent intoxicating even with smoke over top of it.

"My brother, Komi, and my parents." Her voice broke as she watched him stare at the pictures, and then his gaze rose to hers, his eyebrows lowered and worry in his eyes.

She closed the locket and took a step back, away from his concern and caring. Moving to the couch, she sat in the corner and stared out the window at the looming mountains, serene in the distance.

Eli sat at the opposite end of the couch, on the edge, his body angled toward her, all of his attention on her.

He waited, not pushing as she tried to figure out how to share the story. She'd never talked about it with anyone who didn't already know at least some of the details. It had caught the fancy of local news stations and no matter how many *no comment*s she threw at them, they still wrote about it. A personal interest story that was such a mix of triumph and tragedy.

Her fingers rubbed the locket as she said, "My parents didn't support my desire to become a police officer. Not just because they thought it was too dangerous and not just because they thought a woman didn't belong in law enforcement, both of which they did. But mostly because of the history of law enforcement and our community. Both of my parents had been pulled over more than once for DWB. You know, Driving While Black. I wanted to be an officer because I wanted to help people, especially after I saw how police could make a difference for someone in trouble. But I also wanted to be part of the solution, part of the change. They thought I was being a traitor."

She sighed, staring at her lap, all the embittered

words she and her parents had tossed back and forth, all the tension between them, rushing back. A familiar anger and frustration followed, but it was swallowed up by the grief. All that lost time, being angry at one another. She'd run out of time to change their minds. And that wasn't the worst of it.

"When I told them about my graduation from the police academy, they refused to come. I fought them on it, day after day, trying to wear them down. Trying to get them to support me, even if they didn't understand, even if they didn't agree. To put their love for me above their hatred of the system." A sob worked its way up her throat as she said, "It worked. I convinced them. Because they loved me."

Eli scooted closer, moving into the center of the couch. He put his hand on top of her hand that rested on the seat beside her. He didn't squeeze or fit his fingers between hers, just let it sit there, a silent show of support at a level she could handle right now.

She looked up from her lap, focused her gaze on his face, full of concern and sympathy.

Her voice shifted into a monotone, her gaze moving to those mountains, her favorite source of calm. "There was a pileup on the freeway that day. Eighteen cars, and everyone in the first seven vehicles was killed by either the crash or the flammable materials the truck was carrying that ignited. Firefighters didn't get there in time. My parents were in the seventh car." *So* close to the dividing line between who had lived and who had died that day. "They died on their way to my graduation for something they didn't believe in, that I'd *made* them come to."

"Oh, Ava," Eli breathed. "I'm so sorry."

Her lips twisted, a familiar bitterness welling up. "I spent five years on the force in Chicago, trying to prove that I'd chosen a worthwhile profession, that their deaths hadn't been for nothing." Something else those damn reporters had picked up on, tried to turn into a way for them to make money. "Five years trying to convince Komi that I wasn't to blame."

The hand over hers squeezed slightly, and then his fingers did interlock with hers, but instead of feeling like too much, it felt like the anchor she needed. She squeezed back, holding tight.

"Five months ago, I tried calling Komi again. I'd called him every couple of months ever since the accident, left him messages. He rarely answered, and when he did, it was more of the same: he couldn't forgive me." Her voice broke again. "He didn't know if he ever would."

She took a couple of shaky breaths, trying to calm the grief rising up in her chest, tightening her lungs and making the backs of her eyes sting. "This time, he told me to stop calling. Said it was enough, that it was time for both of us to stop trying, to stop pretending. He said that I wasn't his sister anymore."

"You know none of that is your fault," Eli said, his thumb stroking the side of her palm.

She shifted to face him, her lips lifting in an ironic smile. "Intellectually, sure. I didn't cause the ice storm that day. I wasn't driving the truck that slid on the ice that started the pileup. The truck that was carrying flammable materials that ignited when the first car behind it tried to stop and couldn't, slamming into the truck just like sixteen more after that. But that doesn't stop me from feeling guilty every day. And honestly? I'm angry, too."

She'd never admitted that part to anyone before, hadn't even wanted to admit it to herself. Right now, saying it out loud felt freeing. "I'm angry that my brother blames me, when we should have been grieving together."

She took another deep breath, the tension around her heart loosening slightly. "My extended family is all far away. I love them, but I don't see them all that often. My brother is only a year younger than me. We've always been close. We should have supported each other through this time, not had it separate us, too."

"Grief makes people act in irrational ways," Eli said. "Hopefully, someday he'll realize that."

"I hope so," Ava said, her free hand squeezing tight around the locket. "Because in so many ways, it feels like I lost him that day, too."

Eli sat silently for a long moment, maybe sensing that she needed to sit with the impact of her words, with the complexity of her feelings.

Then, he said softly, "I'm sorry you had to go through all of that. You and I don't know each other well yet, but I'm your friend. I want to support you, however you need."

She felt her lips twist a little at the word *friend* and she wondered if he'd seen it, because he shifted a little closer. Words started to form on his lips that she wasn't sure she was ready to hear.

She cut him off, admitted in another confessional rush, "I came here for a fresh start. A way to clear the slate, to not have to see that freeway where my parents died or the reporters on TV who hounded me for months afterward, looking for a story. I thought it would be easier. But I just don't fit in."

Not with anyone besides Lacey, who'd been hurt today because she hadn't realized what Lacey was trying to tell her soon enough. She didn't say those words out loud, because she knew it was more irrational guilt. Even if she owned a part of the blame, she didn't own all of it. She hadn't set the bomb.

"It takes time," Eli said. "Small towns are great in many ways. The sense of community, the way people look out for each other, is unlike anything you'll find elsewhere. But people in small towns can be insular, too. It takes a little time to go from outsider to part of the community."

Ava nodded, appreciating that perspective but knowing part of the problem was her. Her fear of facing more rejection. Her wariness of letting anyone else in who she might lose.

Frustration built inside her that she felt this way, that she feared what she needed most. Connections.

"You were right. I love Lacey. I feel closer to her than anyone. But it's hard to form connections at work when you're not just the outsider, but the one that the Chief thinks could only get along with a dog."

Surprise flitted across Eli's face, followed by a slight

smile. "Ava. The Chief is the biggest supporter of a K-9 program that I know. He has been for his entire career. Before he was chief, he was a K-9 handler himself. Pairing you with Lacey wasn't a punishment. It was an honor. It was his way of saying he believes in you."

As Ava let those words roll around in her mind, surprising and powerful and buoying, Eli added, "It takes a really special person to be a K-9 handler."

She stared at him, seeing the intensity on his face, the strength of his belief in those words. The frustration and guilt she'd been feeling faded, replaced by something new. Something scary, but exciting. Something she'd been waiting for, but had been afraid to reach out and grab.

Before she could lose her courage, Ava leaned across the seat, closing the distance between them. She slid her hand out from underneath his and locked both of her hands around his neck.

She read the flash of surprise on his face, followed by an intense wanting that made desire flutter in her belly.

Then her lips were on his, softly at first, fitting them to his, learning the feel and taste of them. Then harder, encouraging him to meet her tongue at the seam of his lips.

He didn't hesitate, sucking her tongue into his mouth with a passion that made all her nerve endings fire to life, every inch of her skin suddenly oversensitized.

She slid one hand into his hair, holding his head tight against hers, while the other traveled downward, over the bunching muscles in his back. Her tongue kept dueling with his, as she moved closer, the angle on the couch awkward, too much space between them and too many clothes.

His hands bracketed her ribs, then slid downward, over her waist, then digging in at her hips. His lips and tongue kept moving with hers, quickening the pace, the taste of smoke with something sweet underneath.

A moan emerged from her mouth, something desperate and passionate. It surprised her and she lifted her lips from his, pulling back slightly to stare at him.

He gazed back at her, his blue eyes wide and dilated, his lips damp and his pale skin slightly flushed. His breathing was as hard as hers, a mix of desire and surprise still stamped in his gaze.

A fresh wave of emotions flooded her. A desire to throw herself back into his arms, let him sweep her away into an hour or two where nothing mattered but them. A blend of fear and excitement that suddenly she knew exactly what she wanted.

The certainty that this was the wrong move. The wrong time.

She let out a shaky breath and stood. "I shouldn't have done that. We're coworkers. I—we need to keep this professional."

Eli stood more slowly, never taking that smoldering gaze off hers. "We're only truly coworkers until we find that bomber. Once we do, I'm going to pursue you with everything I've got." Then he gave her a wide confident grin.

Even as he stepped away from her, she felt herself swaying toward him. Felt herself falling toward something that seemed inevitable.

Chapter Nineteen

When they stepped out of her dented Charger in the police station's parking lot on Friday morning, Ava glanced around and then her shoulders slumped with obvious relief.

No one was there to see them arriving at the station together, first thing in the morning.

Eli knew he should feel the same way. He didn't want rumors starting and he didn't want Ava to feel uncomfortable, especially after everything she'd shared with him yesterday. Still, he wished she hadn't looked quite so relieved.

He also wished she hadn't been quite so embarrassed after she'd kissed him, or quite so shy the rest of the evening. Not that they'd spent a lot of time together. She'd pointed him to the guest bathroom and he'd showered the smoke off as best he could. He'd tossed his uniform in her washing machine, even though ultimately it would go in the trash. But he'd had nothing else to wear. He'd waited out the washer and dryer time wrapped in a towel and trying to pretend he didn't notice all her furtive glances while they devoured a hastily-warmed frozen pizza together.

Then he'd climbed back up the stairs to her guest bedroom, where he'd passed out until this morning. He'd had her swing by his hotel so he could get a change of clothes, but his vehicle was still in the Jasper PD parking lot.

The drive in to work had been full of slightly awkward small talk. Whenever their gazes locked, she'd start fidgeting. The only time she'd seemed unconcerned about being alone with him was when they'd swung by the vet's office to check on Lacey. For those moments, Ava had been too focused on the dog to look nervous.

They'd found Lacey groggy and clearly in some pain. But she was moving around, walking gingerly and her tail had wagged like mad when she'd seen Ava.

He and Ava had both pet Lacey and praised her until Marie had finally given them an understanding smile and told them Lacey needed a chance to rest some more. Then they'd climbed into Ava's vehicle and she'd slid back into that anxious silence.

Now, she glanced around the empty parking lot one more time and then hurried inside, not giving him a chance to take advantage of the fact that they were alone.

Not that he would have said or done anything in the police station parking lot. No, he'd already told her his plan last night. He understood her desire to press pause on whatever was happening between them while they were working together. But he wasn't giving up.

As soon as he followed her inside, they were surrounded by other members of the department, officers slapping them on the back or checking that they were okay.

Eli nodded, giving praise where it was due: to Lacey for warning them, for physically putting herself in front of him when he hadn't realized what she was saying. He'd thought she'd seen the same figure he had, running for the woods or the shed. In retrospect, had he actually seen a person? Or could it have been an animal, a deer or even a caribou or moose? He wasn't sure.

It had all happened too fast, just a flash of movement and color where it didn't belong. Then, the world around him had exploded. He'd been flying through the air, too quickly to try and protect his face or brace himself for the fall. Then there'd been nothing until Ava's tortured scream woke him, a scream he'd heard in his nightmares last night.

All he knew was that if Lacey hadn't gotten in front of him, making him stop, he would have been running full force toward the shed behind the house when the explosion hit. He probably would have died in Sanderson's yard.

He glanced at Ava, looking flustered by all the attention, and he was overwhelmed by relief. Not just that he hadn't died yesterday, but that he hadn't put her through losing someone else in a fiery blast.

He didn't know her as well as he wanted to yet, but he could tell she blamed herself—at least partially—for not having recognized Lacey's warning sooner. If something had happened to him, he knew she would have done the same second-guessing, especially since she'd encouraged him to stop and think over a plan before arriving. She'd wonder if they should have spent more time planning, more time researching.

The guilt she carried now was unfair, and he ached for her. She'd faced so many losses in such a short time, and all connected to the dream she'd had for herself of being a police officer. What must it be like for her going to work every day with that connection, even if logically she knew she wasn't to blame?

"Hey, Eli, Ava," Jason said as he slid past the group of officers slowly moving back to their own work. "Are you okay?" He put a hand on Ava's arm before they could answer. "I'm so glad Lacey is going to be all right. I talked to Tashya ten minutes ago and she said that Lacey was standing and having some food. She and Marie will take great care of her while she heals."

Ava nodded, her smile genuine, even though she still looked slightly uncomfortable with the attention. "I got to see Lacey this morning before we—before I came in. I'm so relieved."

"You two are okay?" Jason persisted, his gaze going from the bandage on Eli's forehead to the angry red abrasion on Ava's cheek. "Because Brady and I can hold down the fort if you need more time to heal."

"No, we're okay," Ava insisted, tucking her hands, which had large bandages across the tops of them, into her pockets. "Just some cuts and scratches."

It was mostly true. He barely felt the various cuts over his body, besides the deeper one on his thigh, which was a constant dull ache.

She hadn't mentioned the fact that he'd been unconscious briefly, that he was fairly sure she had been as well. Neither of them had gotten checked out, which was probably a mistake. But neither of them had shown any symptoms of a concussion, either, and it had been almost twenty hours since the explosion.

Eli nodded his agreement. "We're ready to dive back into the investigation." He followed Jason and Ava toward the conference room. "What do we know so far?"

"Brady and I headed there as soon as you called it in, but there wasn't a lot we could do besides search the woods and open the shed. Firefighters had to come and put out the blaze before anyone could go near that house. We were on the scene for about eight hours and then Lieutenant Hoover and Sergeant Diaz took over."

When they followed Jason into the conference room, Brady leaped to his feet and hurried over, studying them both as if looking for injuries. "Are you okay? I can't believe Sanderson blew her own house."

Ava nodded as Eli assured Brady, "We're fine. Thanks to Lacey."

"I heard." Brady gave Ava an impressed look. "She's a hero."

"She is," Ava agreed. "Hopefully she'll be back at work in a few weeks."

"There's been no sign of Sanderson since her house exploded?" Eli asked, wondering if there was a chance it hadn't been her but someone else who'd blown the place. Maybe an accomplice who was worried Sanderson was messing things up.

"Nope," Brady said. "She didn't show up for her job last night and her boss said it's strange that she didn't even call in. Apparently, she's his most reliable bartender. He heard about the explosion, assumed it was a gas problem and feared she'd been inside. Cal Hoover was just in here confirming that there was no body in the rubble."

Ava glanced at him, looking unsurprised but troubled.

Sanderson blowing up her own house felt like an end game, or desperation. Had she just overreacted, thinking they had more evidence than they actually did? Or had she spotted them and panicked?

In either case, would she forget her grudge and run far from Jasper? Or hide somewhere and set off another bomb soon?

"I think we'd better start talking to her family and friends," Eli said.

"Did you find anything interesting in the shed?" Ava asked at the same time.

"Just standard garden tools," Jason said.

"Do we have any more on her time in the military?" Eli asked.

Brady shook his head. "I'm waiting for someone to call me back. But you know how it goes with red tape. All they would confirm so far is that she was honorably discharged."

"Well, that's something," Ava said. "But not particularly useful right now."

"Did we learn anything else at the scene?" Eli asked. "What do we know about the bomb?"

"It was a big IED," Brady said. "Nothing like what you found at the warehouse or the sawmill. As you could probably tell, it contained a lot of explosive material. Still, it wouldn't have caused that much damage except it had been placed beside the house's gas boiler in the basement. Looks like the gas line snapped during the explosion and fueled a much bigger explosion. The bomb had both a timer and a remote way to set it off."

Eli frowned. "I don't suppose we know if the timer was set?"

Brady shook his head. "We assume it was detonated remotely, and that the timer hadn't been set yet, but Sanderson must have had iron nerves to live on top of that thing. Or supreme confidence in her bomb-building skills. Because what if something had set it off by accident before she was ready?"

Eli nodded. "Depending what she was using for her remote detonation, that's a definite possibility. Not to mention that it's pretty extreme to put a bomb under your own house. But who knows? Maybe once she set the bomb or bombs in town, she planned to come back to her house and take herself out rather than wait for us to figure out it was her and arrest her."

Ava gave an exaggerated shiver at the idea. "Do we have any thoughts on who might take her in, hide her?"

Brady and Jason shook their heads in unison. "She doesn't have any family here that we could find," Jason said. "Her parents are back in Kansas. I was planning to give them a call today, see if they've heard from her, if they can tell us why she moved to Jasper or if she holds any grudges."

Eli nodded. "Great. Why don't you and Jason do that? Contact her family, and follow up with the Army? If you learn about any friends she's got in the area, maybe pay them a visit. Ava and I can go to Shaker Peak, talk to her boss in person and talk to the other bartenders and servers."

Jason and Brady were nodding in agreement with his plan before he'd even finished sharing it. Ava gave a forced smile and a nod of her own and Eli tried not to react.

It made sense for them to continue pairing together, and let Brady and Jason stay grouped as well. Besides, he wanted to make sure she was okay after what had happened to Lacey. Clearly, she didn't like the idea.

Maybe she just felt awkward, didn't want him to bring up that kiss—that mind-blowing, eye-opening kiss. Or maybe she was worried the two of them working closely together would mean someone seeing there was more happening between them.

Whatever the case, he wasn't about to change his plan now.

He gestured for her to go first, then followed her out of the conference room. As they wove their way back through the bullpen, several other officers stopped them to express their happiness that he and Ava were okay.

He snuck a glance at her as she thanked them, seeing the smile lifting the edges of her lips. Maybe she was finally beginning to realize that she *was* liked here, that this community could easily become *her* community.

He'd planned to help her fit in before, but his determination to keep her in Jasper doubled. He had a long way to go to get past her defenses, even after they'd stopped working together. He may have only known her less than a week, but one thing he knew for sure.

Ava Callan was worth pursuing.

Chapter Twenty

Shaker Peak was as dismal as Ava remembered. From the dim lighting—probably meant to disguise the fact that the counters could have been cleaner—to the chairs that creaked when they moved and the peeling paint on the walls, the whole place seemed depressing. Maybe that was the point. You came in wanting to drink and the atmosphere made you want more.

Glancing around, Ava took in the only patrons there at 9:30 a.m. on a Friday. A middle-aged white man with a thick mustache wearing a suit with his tie askance and staring forlornly into his whiskey at the bar. A Latinx woman in a black dress that looked more appropriate for an evening at a club, scowling in a cracked corner booth. Her stilettos were on the table beside her beer and peanuts.

Behind the bar, a tall, thin Black woman with a series of tattoos on both arms eyed them as she wiped down the counter. "Can I help you?"

Eli stepped forward and Ava couldn't help but notice how assured he looked, no matter whether he was sending a robot into a warehouse to check out a bomb or talking to people in the course of an investigation.

Or when he was telling a woman he planned to pursue her with everything he had. The memory rose Ava's temperature, and she blinked it away, focusing on the here and now.

Eli gave the bartender a friendly smile, lowering his voice as he asked, "Do you know Jennilyn Sanderson?"

Her eyes narrowed, and she glanced from him to Ava. "Why do the cops want to know about Jenny?"

"Your boss didn't say anything to you?" Eli pressed.

Her forehead crinkled, and her expression went from hostile to worried. "He said there'd been an explosion at her house. Some kind of gas leak?" Her hand fisted around the rag, moving rapidly across the counter. "She wasn't home, was she? I haven't heard from her."

"She wasn't home," Ava said.

The bartender let out an audible sigh. "I'm so glad. Do you know why she didn't come in for her shift? I mean, even considering that her house blew up and there are probably things she has to deal with, it's weird that she didn't call. She's shown up to a shift so sick she could barely stand."

"Can we step outside and chat?" Eli asked.

The bartender glanced at the patron at the counter, who was leaning noticeably toward them, trying to eavesdrop. Scowling, she swatted her rag at him. "Mind your own business, John." Then she called into the back, "Pete, I'm taking a cigarette break!"

"Again?" he called back. "Hurry up!"

"Come on." She didn't wait for Pete to take over at the bar, just strode for the entrance, squinting as she moved from the dark bar into the bright sunshine.

"Let's start over," Eli said. "I'm Captain Eli Thorne and this is Officer Ava Callan."

"Sasha," the bartender introduced herself.

"So, Sasha, we need to ask you some questions about Jennilyn. Hopefully your answers will help us find her."

The bartender frowned, glancing between them again. "She's missing?" There was a long pause, then finally she sighed and pulled out a cigarette, lighting up.

"She is," Ava said, resisting the urge to wave a hand in front of her face to dispel the smoke. "We're trying to figure out why. How well do you know her?"

"Well, she started working here about six months ago, when she moved to Jasper. Shaker Peak doesn't really need more than one bartender at a time except on weekends, but Jenny and I always saw each other switching shifts. And we worked together a lot on the weekends." She shrugged, but her movements were jerky, her drags on her cigarette long. "We got to be good friends. I can't believe she's missing. You think something happened to her? Is this connected to the gas leak?"

"We're not sure yet," Eli answered. "What can you tell us about her? Has anything been bothering her lately? Anyone or anything she expressed anger toward?"

"I mean, what do you want to know? Jenny is Jenny. She is opinionated and kind of a badass, if you want to know the truth. No one messes with her. No one messed with me when she was around, either. Because you know, mostly the clientele here aren't interested in anything except drinking, but like every bar, we get the ones who are looking to start a fight. Or the alcohol loosens them up and they decide it's a good idea to harass a woman."

"So, they all knew Jennilyn wouldn't stand for it?" Ava asked. "She was like a bouncer?"

Sasha laughed, an anemic sound that didn't match her much deeper voice. "I guess. I mean, she definitely threw a few guys out on their asses."

"Anyone in particular?" Eli asked.

"Not really. Just whoever needed it. But you know, she used to be in the Army, so she had skills."

Ava shared a discreet glance with Eli. "What kind of skills?"

"She is strong. I mean, she isn't all that big." Looking Ava over, she said, "A few inches shorter than you. But her muscles are killer. Those biceps?" She laughed again. "I don't know how she did that." Sasha flexed her own slender arm, and the muscle barely showed. "Jenny said she didn't even go to a gym. I guess she had lots of weights at home." Her amusement faded at the word *home* and she took another series of drags from her cigarette, shaking the ash onto the street.

"Do you know what she did for the Army?" Eli asked.

Sasha shrugged. "I don't know. What does anyone *do* for the Army? Fight, I guess."

"What about explosives?" Eli persisted. "Did she have any experience with those in the military?"

"Explosives?" Sasha glanced between them, perplexed. Then she shook her head rapidly. "Oh, no. No way. You think Jenny blew up *her own house*? Why the hell would she do that?"

"We're not sure," Ava said carefully. "But there's

some evidence that she might have. Whether or not it was her, it's really important that we talk to her."

Sasha's lips formed a thin line, her cigarette burning low in her hand. Just when Ava thought she was going to have to give more incentive, Sasha said, "Look, I know Jenny has a temper, but this makes no sense. She wouldn't blow anything up, especially her own house! I mean, yeah, she was kind of underwater on the mortgage since she couldn't rely on half the cost from that jerk of an ex. But good riddance. She dumped him, so she knew she was better off owing money than dealing with him, no matter how much he begged. She certainly wasn't so torn up over it that she'd blow the place up to get rid of the memories."

Ava felt Eli's gaze on her as she asked, "What's the ex's name?"

"Dennis something. Dennis… Ryon! That's it. Listen, if you go talking to him, don't believe anything he says about—ow!" Swearing, Sasha dropped her cigarette, which had burned ash down to her fingertips, then stomped it out. Sucking on her fingers, she mumbled, "There's bad blood between him and Jenny."

Tension built inside Ava, an anxiousness to get moving and talk to Dennis Ryon. Maybe he could tell them where Jennilyn might be hiding. Or maybe he was a potential target they needed to warn.

She glanced at Eli, who asked, "One more thing, Sasha. Do you know where Jennilyn might go if she needed a place to hide out?"

"Nah." Sasha scowled as she blew on her fingers. "Look, she was a good friend, but we were mostly work friends, you know? I've never been to her house. We didn't really hang out outside of the bar." She glanced at it, the windows dark with grime, and turned away from them. Over her shoulder she said, "When you find her—and you realize she *didn't* blow up her own house—do me a favor and ask her to call us, okay?"

She didn't wait for an answer, just disappeared back inside.

Chapter Twenty-One

Tracking down Dennis Ryon wasn't easy.

Three hours after they'd left Shaker Peak, Eli pulled his SUV into the parking lot of Salmon Creek Motel, a cheap but clean motel that had sat on the outskirts of Jasper for as long as Eli could remember. Despite the fact that the tourist spot was Salmon River and the motel was nowhere near it, they did a steady business. They rented to the tourists who flocked to the area in the summers and winters, needing a place to stay as they drove from one small town to the next, skiing or swimming. They also rented longer-term, especially in the off-season.

At first, Eli had thought Dennis had left town when he and Jennilyn broke up. Eli and Ava had called Brady and Jason to update them, and have them ask Jennilyn's family about Dennis. Brady had called back twenty minutes later and said that the family had never met Dennis, but it hadn't stopped them from disliking him.

They said Jennilyn had met him during her time in the Army and the two of them got out at the same time. When her family had expected her to finally come back to Kansas and settle down there, she'd announced she and Dennis were moving in together. They wanted to have an adventure, find someplace neither of them had ever been and buy a home. Their only requirements were that the spot be quiet and small. And apparently, somewhere *not* in Kansas.

Dennis and Jennilyn had bought the house together, but because of Dennis's bad credit, hers was the only name on the mortgage. When he left last month—they didn't know what had caused the split—she'd been left with a house she couldn't afford. Still, she wouldn't come home, they'd lamented.

"What impression did you get of the family?" Ava had asked while Eli stared at her.

The bright early morning sun streaming through the windshield had highlighted the way her light brown eyes got a little darker around the edges. It put a glow on her smooth, soft skin, and showed him the slight highlights in her hair, making him want to pull those curls out of the bun, the way they'd been at dinner three nights ago.

She must have sensed him staring, because her gaze had shifted to his, held briefly—just long enough to send a jolt of desire through him—then focused resolutely out the windshield.

"I wasn't impressed with the family," Brady had said. "They didn't come right out and say they wanted her back so she could help them out. But they kept talking about how the Army paid good money and how her loyalty should have been to the people who raised her."

"They didn't seem all that concerned when we said she was missing, either," Jason had added. "They were just angry, like they thought she'd simply left Jasper without telling them where she was going next."

"So, she's probably not in contact with them," Ava had sighed.

"I doubt it." Brady had sounded discouraged as he added, "All they could tell us about where Dennis might be was that they thought he'd gone to stay at a motel. They thought he was biding his time, hoping Jennilyn would take him back. Apparently, the breakup was her decision."

"Did they think she would take him back?" Eli asked.

"Not sure."

After he'd hung up with Brady and Jason, he and Ava had driven around town, working their way outward, checking each of the hotels and motels, and even the camping grounds. The town was small, but since tourism was one of its biggest industries, there was no shortage of places to stay.

After the fifth spot, they'd started making calls instead, trying to get the managers to tell them over the phone if Dennis Ryon was a guest. Some had refused to answer, and he'd marked them down as places to visit in person. Others had just heard *police* and dug through their records. They'd finally gotten lucky with Salmon Creek Motel.

"How do you want to play this?" Eli asked, knowing from the time they'd spent working together that she liked to go in with a plan. Whereas with interviews like this, he'd often play it by ear, let the tone of the conversation lead him to the right tactic.

But he wasn't inflexible. And he wanted her to feel like she had as much say in this investigation as he did.

She twisted toward him, and Eli couldn't stop his gaze from dropping to her lips. She'd shocked the hell out of him when she'd kissed him, but ever since he'd been having trouble focusing on much besides strategizing how to get a repeat.

"Sasha made it sound like Dennis wanted Jennilyn back," Ava said, her tone all-business, so much so that he thought she could read the train of his thoughts.

He gave her a quick grin and her words stalled before she rushed on, "I think we need to be careful not to make it seem like something he tells us could get her in trouble and wreck his chances. But he might have good insight into who she'd hate enough to target with a bomb."

"Agreed. So, the you're-helping-us-help-her angle?"

Ava nodded, reaching for the door. "Yep. Let's do this."

Surprised, he jogged to catch up as she walked toward Room 113. Like all of the rooms, it was accessible from an exterior door. Maybe he was rubbing off on her if she thought that sufficed as their plan. Just like she was rubbing off on him, having him suggest one in the first place.

They made a good team. The thought didn't surprise him, exactly, but it did make his steps slow as he stared at her, striding purposefully toward the motel.

He'd always had a vision of himself, far into the future, sitting on a wraparound porch like the one at Ava's rental, lounging on a glider while a wife—someone whose features were hazy—chatted from a rocking chair beside him. Right now, he could picture Ava on that rocker, Lacey by her side while Bear laid at his feet.

Shaking the image clear—it was *way* too soon for that kind of daydream—he hurried after her again as she knocked forcefully on the door of Room 113.

The man who answered looked about her age. His blondish-brown hair was sheared short, like he was still in the Army, and his biceps—displayed beneath a sleeveless T-shirt—were well-developed. Only the slight paunch at his waistline suggested he'd fallen off the Army routine.

He frowned from Ava to Eli, slight nerves underneath the confusion, a common reaction to a police visit. "Can I help you?"

Eli stepped up beside Ava. "Dennis Ryon?" When he nodded, Eli said, "We wanted to chat with you about Jennilyn Sanderson."

The frown deepened, but there was something in his hazel eyes—a hint of glee, like he was happy to have any reason to talk about her. "She get in another bar fight and want me to bail her out?"

"Not exactly," Ava said. "Have you spoken to her friends or family recently?"

Dennis's frown shifted into a scowl. "No. Jenny and I broke up a month ago." He shrugged, but it was forced, angry. "She'll change her mind. She always does. But she didn't get along with her family, so I never really talked to them. And I haven't talked to her *friends*."

He spit the last word out in a way that made Eli want to dig deeper, but Ava pressed forward. "I hate to be the one to tell you, but her house exploded earlier today. She's fine," Ava rushed on, "but we have reason to believe Jennilyn is the one who blew it."

Dennis's eyes widened and he glanced back and forth between them with surprise, but his lips trembled.

Suppressed amusement? Fear? Eli wasn't sure.

He studied the six-foot tall white man more closely, trying to read him. Dennis definitely had conflicting emotions when it came to Jennilyn—love and anger and frustration all blended together. Would it be enough to make him help them, either out of revenge or in order to try and help his ex? Or would it go the other way, make Dennis close off?

When Dennis finally spoke, his tone was careful, modulated. "Why would Jenny blow up her house? I mean, I know she was mad about the cost after we broke up, but what was I going to do, keep paying when I wasn't living there? Besides, she loved that place. We checked out a lot of little towns before we landed here. Jasper was *her* idea. I would have kept looking. I mean, no offense, but this place could have a *few* more job opportunities, right?"

When neither of them answered, he sighed. "Look, I don't know why you think Jenny would blow up the house. But no way."

His words were confident, but the way he glanced back and forth between them, like he was trying to convince them, wasn't.

"She had bomb-making knowledge from the Army, though, right?" Eli guessed.

"Well, yeah." Dennis shoved his hands into the pockets of his loose jeans. "So what? And look, I know she's got…anger issues, but that doesn't mean she'd *blow something up*!"

"What kind of anger issues?" Ava asked.

His eyebrows lifted. "I thought you knew about the bar fight. And the time she smashed up that guy's car with a fricking baseball bat. But she's never used a bomb." He glanced back and forth between them again, like he hoped they were buying it.

"Who else is she angry with, Dennis?" Ava asked softly.

"No. No, I don't… I'm not helping you get her in trouble."

"Maybe you're helping her stay out of it," Eli said.

He stared at the ground a moment, and Eli nodded at Ava, telling her silently to wait him out.

Finally, he looked up, his jaw tight, but with that same suppressed happiness in his gaze, like he believed this could be his ticket back into Jennilyn's life. "Maybe the owner of the bar? She always said he was spineless, that he wouldn't stand up to anyone who was causing trouble at the bar. That she had to take care of the low-lifes herself."

Eli nodded, catching Ava's concern from the corner of his eye. "Who else?"

"I don't know. Maybe the bank? She was pissed that they used my credit score as an excuse to try and give us a high interest rate. She didn't want to go on the mortgage alone. I didn't want that, either," Dennis said quickly. "But she was really mad about it. She used to complain about the loan officer all the time."

"What bank?" Eli asked. "Do you know the loan officer's name?"

"Jasper Financial was the bank. You know, the one out by all those furniture stores? I don't remember the guy's name, but he wore these ridiculous plaid suits every time we met with him. You can't miss him if you go in there."

Ava nodded. "Is there anyone else you can think of?"

When he shook his head, Eli asked, "What about somewhere Jennilyn might be staying? A friend's house or maybe a hotel under a different name? Or squatting or camping somewhere?"

Dennis frowned, shook his head tightly. "I don't know."

"Are you sure?" Ava pressed. "Because if we can find her, maybe we can stop her from doing something she can't undo."

The words hung in the air a long time, but when Dennis's gaze locked on first Ava, then Eli, it was hard. "I'm sure."

Chapter Twenty-Two

"You think Dennis knows where Jennilyn is staying?" Eli asked, glancing at Ava in the passenger seat.

They'd called Brady and Jason, who were headed to the bank now. He and Ava were taking the bar, which in his mind was the more likely target. Normally, he'd ask the other team members to take the closer spot, but since he had the most bomb experience, this plan seemed best.

"I don't know." Her brow was furrowed, her fingers tapping a rapid beat against the display in his center console. "He acted different when we asked where she was. Angry, almost. Like he knew she was at a friend's house when she could have come stayed with him? When he talked about her friends was the only other time he seemed *mad*."

"You noticed that, too, huh?"

"Yeah. I didn't want to get distracted with his hang-ups. Given the way Sasha talked about Dennis, it seems like that was a mutual feeling. I doubt his dislike of her friends will tell us anything about her next target."

"If Sasha is such a good friend, you think Jennilyn would actually target the bar? Risk killing her?"

It had been bothering Eli ever since they'd gotten back in the SUV. Captain Rutledge's description of Jennilyn during the bar fight, combined with the way Sasha and Dennis had talked about how she jumped into action there, made the grudge against the bar owner seem the strongest. If the bombing was a planned escalation of the violence she'd shown before—against men harassing women in the bar and a man who'd assaulted her friend—someone who sat back and let that kind of behavior happen, in a *place* that was also a likely spot for trouble, seemed a good potential target. Still, he wasn't sure Jennilyn would risk hurting a friend in the process.

"She might know Sasha's schedule," Ava suggested. "Or she could have set a bomb to blow after the place was closed. Take out the owner's livelihood without actually planning to endanger anyone?"

"Maybe," Eli mused, hoping Ava was right. "She *did* smash up that guy's car instead of taking the baseball bat to his head. And even though she put someone in the hospital during the bar fight, it was a broken leg. Not a broken neck."

Ava nodded, catching his eye as he glanced at her. "True. She probably has the training to have done worse."

"Why graduate to bombs?" Eli wondered. "Why try to scare the town if her targets are specific?"

"I don't know," Ava said as he pulled up to the bar, which had a few more cars parked in the lot now that it was lunchtime. "Maybe we were wrong about that. Maybe it was just where she was practicing with the materials."

"Then why leave them behind where someone could

find them? I mean, it's not like she was nervous having them nearby if she'd set her own home to blow."

Ava gave him a worried look as they both hopped out of the SUV. "We're definitely missing something."

"Why don't you talk to the owner while I start checking the place out?" Eli suggested.

"Let's do this," Ava agreed, her stride purposeful.

As she walked through the back door, holding it open for him to grab behind her, Eli glanced around, searching for any sign of Jennilyn lurking.

The skin on the back of his neck prickled, his shoulders coming up as an image of the house exploding formed. The gash on his leg ached with the memory, and his breathing came faster, thinking of the movement he'd seen in the trees.

It wasn't just his life on the line, but Ava's, too. He'd been the one running for the trees, running for whoever might have been hiding there. Like he always was, decisive when he chose a course of action. Relying on his instincts.

In the close to a decade he'd been a police officer, those instincts had never steered him wrong. The officers he worked with trusted his gut as much as he did. But Ava had been behind him yesterday. Too close behind him.

Had Jennilyn blown the house when she knew they'd be injured but would be unlikely to be killed? A warning to back off? Or had she misjudged, meant to end his and Ava's investigation for good? Could she be trying to track them now, looking for another chance?

He saw no one on the street besides a young woman

pushing a stroller. Ignoring the anxiety churning in his gut, he followed Ava inside.

Blinking to adjust to the dim lighting, he paused at the doorway, glancing around, looking for possible hiding spots for a bomb, while Ava strode right for the bar counter.

The woman behind the bar—a reed-thin white woman with bright red hair—watched her approach, frowned as Ava asked for the owner, then waved her behind the bar and into the back room.

In the main part of the bar, the patron who'd been there that morning was still at the counter. Now, his elbows were perched on the wood, his shoulders stooped downward, his chin almost resting on his collection of empty glasses in a variety of sizes. The woman who'd been in the corner booth was gone, but a group of men sat in the center of the room, their conversation loud and obnoxious, a mix of beer bottles and shot glasses on their table.

"You wanna join us, cop?" one of them called to him as his buddies laughed.

Ignoring them, Eli circled the edges of the room first, peering under tables and behind the old pinball machine that looked like it hadn't worked in a decade. Spots that would be easy to slide a bomb underneath while walking through a room. Jennilyn could have carried it in her purse, then tacked it to the underside of a table when she sat down for a break. Or she could have put it somewhere harder to access, less likely to be spotted even if someone fell down—not an unlikely occurrence in a place like this. Perhaps she'd set it while the bar was empty and she was the only worker.

The group of men watched him for less than a minute, calling out questions about what he was looking for, then voicing pseudo-whispered insults about what it might be. Finally, they gave up on getting his attention and went back to drinking.

Only the bartender continued to track his movements with narrowed eyes. When he reached the bar, she asked, "What are you looking for?" From the nervous way she scrubbed at the counter with a rag, he suspected Sasha might have told her about the bomb.

"Us being here is just a precaution," Eli said, meeting her gaze with a confident, relaxed expression. There was no reason to panic anyone. Especially since, so far, there was no sign of a bomb.

"Your partner is in the back," she said as Eli moved behind the bar, checking the shelves beneath the counter, between bottles.

His partner. For now, it was true. He wanted to find the bomb, find Jennilyn and end this case soon, so he could ask Ava out. But he also enjoyed the day-to-day with Ava, working beside her. She was a good officer, a good K-9 handler. She was insightful and thorough, and although he loved the thrill of jumping into a new day, not knowing what challenge would be thrown at him, he also appreciated her more cautious, methodical approach. He even liked the simple, companionable silence of riding with her to a scene. He was going to miss everything about partnering with her when he returned to McCall.

He glanced toward the double swinging doors that led into the back room, then refocused on the shelves full of bottles. He peered inside each one, making sure Jennilyn hadn't emptied one out and slid a compact pipe bomb inside. It was tedious, and dust rose up from many of the bottles, making his nose itch. Each one gave the telltale slosh of liquid as he investigated.

His shoulders came down with each inch he searched that revealed nothing. The right-sized bomb could easily be hidden, and in a workplace where others could stumble upon it and destroy her plan, Eli was sure Jennilyn would have picked a good spot.

As he reached the end of the bar, Eli glanced around once more, making sure he hadn't missed anything. He was about to move into the back room when Ava pushed open the swinging door, almost knocking him down with it.

"Sorry," she said, her eyes wide as she spotted him right on the other side. Then she shook her head. "Nothing there."

"You sure?"

"Oh, yeah. I checked everything, not that there's a whole lot. They don't serve food here beyond peanuts and chips, so there are basically storage cupboards and a desk in the corner stacked with papers. It's much tinier than you'd think, but I also looked in the closet where you can access electrical. Nothing."

Eli frowned. "What about the owner? Did you tell him we wanted to check out the exterior of his house?"

Ava nodded. "Yeah. He has no interest in coming with us, but says to knock ourselves out. I suggested he change the locks at the bar, but he doesn't want to waste the money."

Eli sighed. Noticing that the bartender was listening in, he nodded toward the back door. The group of men in the center of the room had plenty to say as Ava passed and she shook her head at him as she strode right on by, ignoring them all.

His jaw clenched and he gave them his most aggressive warning look as he followed her outside.

Before he had a chance to ask how she didn't look furious at the filth they'd spewed at her, she said, "If this is her target, she still has access. She could slip in at night and leave a bomb. Maybe we'll get lucky at his house—she does seem like the kind of person who'd want to be specific about her target—but I'm worried, Eli."

"Me too," he agreed, thinking of all of Jennilyn's potential targets. All the different types of bombs she could have encountered working for the Army. Not to mention all of the knowledge she would have gained about how to ambush someone when they least expected it. "I think we need to stop chasing where she could have *been* and find a way to track where she is *now*."

Chapter Twenty-Three

"No sign of a bomb anywhere," Eli said as he hung up the phone with Brady.

Ava frowned as she slid into the passenger seat of his SUV, exhausted and filthy from searching the exterior of the bar owner's house—including under the deck. Mosquito bites itched on the back of her neck and, inexplicably, on her legs covered by her uniform.

Eli looked worse than she felt, his light skin caked in a layer of dirt, his hair sticking up. His uniform, black just like the Jasper PD uniforms, was so dust-covered that even the dark color couldn't disguise it.

All for nothing. If Jennilyn was targeting the owner of Shaker Peak, she was biding her time.

"Brady and Jason checked the bank *and* the loan officer's house?"

"Yep," Eli confirmed. "His car, too."

Ava nodded, remembering how Eli had circled the bar owner's car in the lot, looking underneath with a retractable mirror. Finding nothing there, either.

Day had slid into evening as they'd searched, getting nowhere and losing time. Time for Jennilyn to hunker down deeper wherever she was hiding. Time for her to come up with a new plan or set a bomb somewhere they hadn't considered.

Ava sighed, glancing at Eli from the corner of her eye as he put the SUV in gear, at the lean muscles in forearms revealed by the rolled sleeves of his uniform. Even covered in dirt, there was something compelling about him, something that made her gaze want to linger.

He looked at her, giving her a slow grin that crinkled the corners of his eyes, before returning his attention to the road.

He'd glanced at her while they'd worked quietly at the bar owner's house, too. Quick, probing glances like he was trying to go deeper than she'd already let him in, sharing the most painful parts of her past with him as if she'd known him for years instead of just a week.

Seven days. It seemed impossible that she hadn't known him longer. The proximity, the pressure of the investigation, was making everything intensified. But it was more than that. Almost like pieces of her lined up just right with pieces of him, a mix of similar and opposite that felt like they belonged together.

Inevitable. It was what she'd felt after she'd kissed him, after she'd stepped back and he'd let her press pause, hadn't pressured her for more. After he'd promised to give her time, but not to give up.

A shiver of anticipation slid through her as she darted one more glance at him. She wanted this investigation over *now*, wanted to experience the thrill of whatever it meant to be pursued by everything Eli Thorne had.

Too soon, she reminded herself. Even if it wasn't, she wasn't making the same mistakes twice. Wasn't going to risk alienating colleagues she'd barely started to connect with for the *possibility* of a relationship.

Maybe what she really needed was for this investigation to drag on and on, give her a chance to get to know him better. Maybe then she'd realize it was attraction without enough common ground, something that would sizzle out as fast as it had ignited.

But as she felt his gaze on her again, as she forced her own gaze to remain steady out the window, she knew that was just the fear talking. The worry that she'd fall too hard and he'd walk away. That he'd be one more person who left her all alone.

The buzzing of her phone startled her, tickling her leg. She pulled it out of her pocket, her pulse jumping when she saw Emma Daniels's name. "Emma," she answered in a rush. "Have you heard something about Lacey?"

The German shepherd had looked fine when they'd stopped by that morning, but Ava knew how quickly medical prognoses could change. When her parents died, she'd known she should avoid the news coverage. She'd tried, but she hadn't been able to deny herself the agony of knowing what they'd experienced, in their final attempt to support her. She'd heard about the couple in the car behind her parents, admitted to the hospital but expected to be fine. A few days in the hospital, though, and instead of being released, the woman had a setback. She'd lived but a closed head injury meant she'd never be the same.

She shivered at the memory, at how hard she'd tried to convince everyone she was fine. While the reporters had hounded her at home, she'd insisted she was able to start work as a police officer. The job she'd known she wanted since she was fifteen and an officer had talked a friend of hers down from the ledge of a building they'd snuck inside together. Her, having no idea of her friend's true intention. The officer, so calm and steady, taking an hour of his life to make sure her friend kept his. The job she'd still chosen to pursue, even with her parents' disapproval, even after their deaths.

Eli's hand closed around hers, jolting her back to the present, and she realized Emma had been talking. "Is Lacey okay?" she repeated, because she hadn't heard whatever Emma had been saying.

There was a brief pause and then Emma said quickly, "She's fine, Ava. I talked to Marie a couple of hours ago and she was doing great."

A huge relieved breath escaped and Ava nodded at Eli, who squeezed her hand. She blinked back the tears that had been gathering and tried to focus on Emma while her fingers twitched, still linked with Eli's.

"If anything happened, Marie would call you first," Emma assured her. "I was just calling to see how *you* were doing."

Warmth speared Ava's chest, the feeling that she'd forged more bonds here than she'd realized. "Thank you. I'm doing okay. Just a little stressed. It's weird not to have Lacey with me on calls."

As she said it, she realized how true it was. She'd had a human partner back in Chicago. She and Shaun had gotten along fine, and she'd trusted him to have her back, but they hadn't been friends. Their bond had been one of necessity. If he was out for a day and she had a different partner, she'd never felt as if she were missing anything.

Now, as much as she enjoyed working with Eli—far more than she'd expected, and not just because she was attracted to him—she constantly found herself glancing down by her side, expecting Lacey to be there. Feeling a pang of disappointment when she wasn't.

"She'll be back before you know it," Emma predicted. "In the meantime…are you still working with that handsome captain?"

A flush of heat speared up Ava's face and she darted a quick glance at Eli, hoping he couldn't hear her conversation.

He was staring out the windshield, seemingly oblivious. But the hand still locked with hers squeezed when she looked his way.

Redirecting her gaze, Ava kept her tone neutral as she said, "Yes, we're working now, actually."

"Ohhh." Emma's voice was teasing as she said, "I'll let you get back to that, then. Say hi to the captain for me."

"Nope," Ava said, refusing to rise to the bait.

Emma laughed and when Ava hung up, Eli asked, "Lacey's okay?"

"Yes. It was just Emma, checking on me."

"That was nice," Eli said as he pulled into the police station parking lot.

Ava glanced around, spotting Captain Rutledge striding through the lot with a take-out cup from Millard's Diner, and the Chief grinning at something Theresa Norwood was saying to him by the entrance.

Ava was suddenly hyperaware of the hand still entwined with Eli's, and discomfort wormed through her. Still, when he slid his hand free, she immediately missed it.

Stepping out of the car, she lifted her hand to wave at Arthur, but he slipped into the station as if he hadn't noticed.

The Chief glanced up when they stepped out of the vehicle, his eyebrows raised.

Ava belatedly brushed her hands over her uniform, dislodging a cloud of dust that made her cough but probably didn't do much for her appearance.

"How'd it go today?" he asked as Theresa nodded hello to them, then headed inside.

Ava shook her head. "No luck."

The Chief glanced from her to Eli and back again. "Can I have a word, Officer Callan?"

"I'll meet you inside," Eli told her, giving her an encouraging smile as nerves tensed Ava's stomach. "Sure, Chief. What is it?"

"Well, first off, how is Lacey?"

The nerves eased up a little. "She'll be okay. Thank goodness."

"Good. I called Marie myself to check on her, but a handler knows their dog best. You and Lacey make a good team."

The compliment made her smile and she remembered Eli's words about it being a show of confidence that the Chief had partnered her with Lacey. "Thank you for pairing me with her."

He nodded, something knowing in his gaze. "I actually wanted to chat with you about something else. I know you haven't had a chance to go on a call with Captain Rutledge yet, but you've worked with him some since you've come to Jasper. How has that gone?"

"Oh." The question felt disconnected with everything in her life right now, and Ava tried to come up with a response that would be honest without being rude. "He seems to know the town well. He's really smart about police procedure."

The Chief's lips turned downward a little, his eyes narrowing. "He is, at that. But what about his personal skills? Working with officers, with the public? This is between us," he added.

"Well, I haven't been here that long," Ava hedged. "I'm sure keeping some distance can help with retaining authority in a small town."

A hint of a smile quivered on the Chief's lips. "I appreciate your diplomacy, Ava. And I get it. Thanks for your insights."

He turned and headed for his personal vehicle before she could ask why he'd wanted her insight in the first place. Over his shoulder, he called, "No overtime, Officer Callan. I want you rested. This investigation could last a while and I need you fresh tomorrow and the next day, too. Not just working yourself into exhaustion tonight in hope of a break."

"Yes, sir," she answered, glancing at the time on her phone as she hurried into the station. Technically, her shift was already over.

"Everything okay?" Eli asked when she jogged into the conference room.

She nodded as she glanced around, finding the room empty except for the two of them.

"We just missed Brady and Jason. The Chief sent them home." He smiled sheepishly. "According to Captain Rutledge, who just passed through here, the Chief wants us to call it a night, too."

"Yeah, he told me." She shrugged. "I get it, and I could definitely use a shower, but I'm anxious. I don't like feeling that we're a step behind. We have to be missing a target."

"We're probably not going to come up with it tonight, though," Eli said, sounding more agreeable to the idea of calling it a night than she felt.

Maybe some of it was simply that she wasn't ready to say goodnight to Eli yet, to go home to her quiet, empty house.

"You want to get some food? I bet Millard's Diner would let us sit on their patio, even covered in dirt."

Even though she'd just been thinking that she wanted to spend more time with him, Ava couldn't stop herself from glancing out the open door of the conference room, hoping no one had overheard.

Eli gave her a half smile that didn't quite meet his eyes. "I'd have invited the whole team if they were still here."

"Oh." She shuffled her feet. "Yeah, of course." She fought an internal battle—wanting all the time with him she could get, but not wanting the rumors that were bound to start if the two of them showed up together at the cop hangout.

Then, she pushed down her anxiety. Yes, her workplace romance with DeVante had fallen apart more publicly than she would have liked. But if she truly wanted a new start, she needed to stop letting the past hinder her from making connections.

She nodded, that quick movement feeling like a big step in the right direction. "Let's go."

Eli grinned, this time a real smile that made creases appear in the dirt alongside his eyes.

She couldn't stop her own smile in return, her pulse picking up. Somehow, in the week she'd known Eli, he'd helped her form a totally different vision of what her future in Jasper could be. With every moment that passed, she sensed he was going to be a big part of it.

Chapter Twenty-Four

Millard's Diner was quieter than usual for a Friday night at the end of a shift. Normally, there would be a group of cops grabbing their last coffee of the day or stopping for a burger before they headed home. Today, there was only a group of teenage girls in a big booth, who stopped giggling long enough to gawk at Ava and Eli as they walked inside, still covered in dirt.

Relief loosened Ava's shoulders, but she realized it wasn't because there were no colleagues to see her out alone with Eli. It was because they wouldn't feel pressured to invite anyone to join them. She'd get Eli to herself a little longer.

She looked at him, a couple of inches taller than her, his arms loose at his sides in that stance that made him seem relaxed no matter the situation. He'd told her about his dog, about feeling connected to his community so much that he'd known he was going to spend his life there. She wanted to know *more*.

She wanted to know if he was close to his family, what he did with his friends. She wanted to know about his hobbies and how he had gotten into bomb detection. She wanted to know *everything*.

When he glanced at her, seeming to sense her gaze, she gave him a slight smile, suddenly overwhelmed by the intensity of her feelings. Then, she turned back to the owner, standing behind the bright blue counter in the retro diner, waiting for their order.

Millard Jr. looked them over with raised eyebrows. "You look like you had a long day. Coffee?" he asked as his wife, Vera, scowled at them from the corner.

"And a couple of burgers," Ava said, glancing at Eli for confirmation. He nodded and she added, "We'll eat them at a table outside."

Vera's scowl eased, but she kept watching them as they turned for the door. Ava glanced back before she stepped outside, and tried not to laugh at Vera's intent stare. She'd overheard some of the younger cops joking that they liked to place bets on whether anyone could get her to smile.

Settling into a small two-person table right outside of Millard's, almost on the sidewalk, Ava stared at Eli. She could tell he was tired by the way he leaned back in his chair with a sigh, but his bright blue eyes always seemed alert and focused. Right now, they were completely focused on her.

Even though they were filthy, sitting outside of a cop hangout, tonight suddenly felt more like a date than even their dinner on the romantic terrace at Rose Café. Maybe it was because she knew him better now, or because she'd kissed him, or because he'd stated his intent to pursue her. He'd promised to wait, but right now, she didn't want to wait for anything.

The idea made her feel lighter, almost giddy, but

she ducked her head so he wouldn't get an idea of what she was thinking. Wanting something didn't mean she should act on it. Then again, once he was back in McCall, maybe it was far enough away that no one would care. Was it really so important to put up artificial boundaries while they were on this case? Or was now the perfect time to push the boundaries, to see what this attraction could turn into, while he was right here in front of her?

"Here you go."

Ava started at Millard Jr.'s voice, then nodded her thanks as he set two cups of coffee on a tray with sugar and creamers in the center of the table.

"Burgers will be up shortly," he called over his shoulder as he ambled back inside.

Then, Ava met Eli's gaze, saw the surprise there at what she must have been telegraphing. "Tell me more about yourself, Eli."

He sat straighter, keeping his gaze locked on hers in a way that made anticipation tighten her belly. "Feels like a first date. I wish I'd cleaned up better."

His tone was joking, giving her an out, but she nodded. "Yeah, me, too. But maybe this is better. Share it all now, the good and the ugly, and see where it takes us."

He gave her one of those slow grins that was somehow sexy even with the dirt ground into his face. "Where should I start?"

She leaned forward, settling her chin on her fist. "Tell me more about your family." Somehow, she knew he was close to them. She could only imagine him as part of a tight-knit family, not one that argued as much as hers had.

"Well, I told you that my parents have been together since they were kids. The whole family lives in or around McCall. I've got two younger brothers, Benjamin and David. Ben just got engaged a couple of weeks ago. I'm hoping I'll be back in McCall before their engagement party at the end of the month."

She nodded, although the idea of him leaving, even a few weeks from now at the end of May, put a hollow feeling in her stomach. "Are your brothers in law enforcement, too?"

"No. But my mom was, until I was a teenager. It's the reason I wanted to do it. Ben and David stuck close to the system, too. Ben is a social worker and David is finishing his law degree."

"Wow." Ava tried to imagine a world where most of her family had jobs that intertwined. A stab of jealousy hit at the easy comradery he seemed to have with his family, but she pushed it aside, glad that Eli had those strong bonds. It was probably part of what made him the way he was, so generous and friendly.

"What about your dad?"

"He's a carpenter," Eli said. "It's funny, because even though my brothers and I gravitated toward careers connected to what my mom did, we all do some woodworking in our spare time."

"Really?" An image of Eli working with his hands, sanding down an old table, covered in sweat and sawdust, filled her mind. She glanced at those hands, with their long nimble fingers that had been so sure working the controls of his bomb-disposal robot. The remembered feel of those fingers digging into her hips while she'd kissed him made her skin tingle.

His head tilted slightly, the hint of a grin playing on his lips, like he could read the direction of her thoughts.

"Why bomb detection?" she blurted, trying to focus on getting to know him better and not her daydreams.

He laughed. "Total fluke. I heard about this program the FBI put on—teaching law enforcement officers around the country some of the most cutting-edge techniques—and I thought it sounded fun." He shrugged. "It was."

Before she could ask more, he said, "What about you? What made you want to become a cop?"

"When I was fifteen, I had this one friend. I'd always get into trouble with him. Stupid stuff, trespassing and things like that. I was just testing boundaries, trying to express my independence." She shrugged, remembering the thrill of sneaking out, of getting in somewhere she wasn't supposed to be. Looking back on it, it all seemed silly and potentially dangerous. Then, it had felt like a slice of freedom from a house with too many rules.

"My friend was trying to escape. I knew his home life was bad, but I didn't realize quite how bad until we snuck into this building downtown. He went out the window, and when I thought we were going to sit out there together and look out over the city, he told me to go home. I realized he was going to jump."

Eli cursed under his breath.

"I went outside, anyway. I've never been afraid of heights, but knowing what he planned to do…" She'd been terrified. "I knew he'd never jump with me watching. He was too good a friend. And he didn't. I called the police while he cried and begged me to leave. They came and one of them spent an hour talking to him, promising to help."

"Wow," Eli said softly.

"Yeah. Back then, I didn't know how tough it was to intervene in domestic violence situations, how hard it is to make that stick in any meaningful way. Back then, both of us just believed him. Somehow, he got it done. Showed up at my friend's house and before I knew it, my friend was moving in with an aunt across the country. I missed him, but he'd write me and I could tell what a better place he was in. Anyway, that day, I decided that I was going to become a police officer."

"It's one of the things I like best about being in law enforcement—helping the community. That invisible thread that ties us all together, if we let ourselves be bound to it."

Ava smiled. "I never quite thought about it like that." To her, being a cop was about helping people, but even in Chicago, where she'd felt like part of a team, she'd never had that bigger connection. She'd never felt like the whole city was in something together. Especially with her parents seeing anyone in blue as the enemy— and it was a perspective she understood, even if she didn't share it. Maybe in a smaller town like Jasper, where there was a real possibility of her eventually knowing most of the people who lived here person-ally, she'd have that feeling someday.

"What—"

The ringing of Ava's phone cut Eli off. She pulled

it out to silence it as Vera silently dropped the burgers off at their table, but then she saw the caller. "Komi," she whispered, unable to believe it.

Her heart started thundering in her ears. Had something happened to someone in their extended family? After everything Komi had said five months ago, she couldn't imagine him calling for any other reason.

Saying a silent prayer, Ava answered. She heard the fear in her own voice as she said, "Komi? What happened?"

Eli's hand reached across the table and she put her free hand in his, taking the support and holding on. In the back of her mind, it registered how natural and easy it felt to rely on him.

"Ava," her brother said, his voice soft and serious.

When the pause dragged on, Ava insisted, "What happened? What's wrong?"

"Wrong? Nothing." Komi sighed. "Look, Ava, I know after everything I said…"

Her pulse slowed a little at the realization that no one was hurt, then took off again. Was it possible he was calling to forgive her?

"I know…" He let out a low laugh, so unlike her decisive brother, and her heart ached just hearing his voice again. "I know I've been unfair to you. I know it's not really your fault that Mom and Dad died." Another pause, then he rushed on, "And it's not right of me to blame you for it. I just—I can't help it. I still don't know if I can get over it, if we can ever go back to where we were. But…"

"But what?" she pressed when he went quiet again,

as hope burst inside of her, almost painful in its intensity.

"I miss you, Ava. I really miss you."

"I miss you, too," she said as tears blurred her vision and Eli squeezed her hand, his smile the only thing she could see.

"That's it," he said with a laugh. Then, more serious, he added, "It's all I've got right now, Ava. But when you left Chicago, I realized that for all the time I'd spent pushing you away, I still expected you to *be there*, to be nearby in Chicago, even if we weren't talking. Even if we never talked again."

The idea made her heart pinch, even though she'd resigned herself to it when she'd moved to Jasper.

"I know how unfair everything I'm saying is, Ava. I'm truly sorry that I can't just snap my fingers and feel differently, no matter how badly I wish I could. No matter how much I know, logically, that you've been grieving as much as I have."

Maybe even more, Ava thought but didn't say. Komi was her little brother. He might have been only a year younger, but she'd always felt responsible for looking after him, for keeping him safe.

When her parents had died, she hadn't just wanted to be the strong big sister for him— she'd also needed that role for herself. Without it, all she'd had was her grief.

"I wanted to hear your voice," Komi said. "I wanted to see if there was a path for us to start fresh. For us to *try*. I still need some space," he added before she could agree. "But I wanted you to know that I do miss you. I miss us together, as a family. I love you, Ava."

"I love you, too," she whispered, closing her eyes at the joy of it.

She'd given up on Komi when she'd moved to Jasper. Given up on ever having that sibling bond back. Given up on the life she'd built for herself in Chicago, so she could avoid the constant, painful reminders of losing her entire family—one way or another—all at once.

This was a small step, but it was so much more than she'd expected, five years after her parents had died. Five months after Komi had completely given up trying, given up the false starts and the angry undercurrents that had plagued every conversation they'd had since their parents' deaths.

Now, suddenly, returning to the life she'd left behind felt like a possibility again.

Chapter Twenty-Five

"There's something about this situation with Jennilyn Sanderson that's bothering me," Ava spoke into the silence.

Eli nodded, in full agreement, even though this wasn't what he wanted to discuss. He wanted to talk about the drastic change in mood that had happened as soon as Ava's brother had called.

He was happy for her. From the way she'd teared up and the excited disbelief that had flashed across her face, he'd known even before she'd told him what her brother had said. He'd also realized what she hadn't said: if Komi could forgive her, she would probably be moving back to Chicago.

He'd never see her again. There was no sense pursuing something when they lived in different states. Not when he couldn't ever imagine leaving the community he had in McCall. Not when her ties to Chicago were pulling on her so strongly. He couldn't imagine a future where either of them would be happy living away from the places they wanted to call home.

So, where did that leave them? To get to spend any time with her would probably be worth the heartache.

But damn, he didn't *want* the heartache, didn't want to start something he knew he'd regret when it ended.

Judging by the way she'd shifted from flirtatious and inquisitive to pensive and work-minded after ending the call with her brother, she felt the same way.

At least he knew *now*, instead of after he and Ava had let things get any further. Because there was no doubt in his mind, if he let Ava Callan in, he'd never want to let her go.

But it was hard to feel relieved when all he wanted to do was pull her into his arms and try to convince her to stay.

"I'm just not sure what it is," Ava said, and Eli tried to focus.

It took him a minute to remember what she was talking about. "Right. Jennilyn Sanderson. Something does feel off. I'm not sure what it is, either."

"I know we're supposed to be off duty." Ava scrunched her lips as she admitted, "The Chief insisted that we not have any overtime. But I've got this itchy feeling like we're missing something important. I don't want to leave it until tomorrow."

Handing some cash to Vera, Eli waved Ava off when she tried to pay for hers. "We could swing by the bar," Eli suggested. "It's a relatively short walk from here. Ask about the friend who she smashed up that guy's car for. It was someone who worked with her, right?"

"Yeah." Ava swore. "You don't think it was the woman who was bartending when we were there earlier, do you? I was so focused on searching for a bomb that it didn't occur to me to talk to her. I was just trying to avoid her listening in and spreading rumors, spreading panic."

"Yeah," Eli agreed. "That was an oversight on both our parts. But at the time, getting to the bar owner's house was more important."

"Let's remedy that now," Ava replied, jumping up and striding in the direction of the bar.

Eli followed more slowly, watching the determination in her steps, the curls that had started to slip loose at the back of her bun. He tried to match her purposeful energy, but there was a weight on his chest he couldn't shake, the knowledge that something amazing had slipped away from him before he'd even fully grabbed hold.

Normally, he'd fight. Continue to find ways to integrate her into the community. Find ways to make her want to stay.

But he knew how much her relationship with her brother meant to her, how much she missed him. Eli couldn't begrudge her the chance to get that back, no matter what it cost him.

"Shake it off," Eli muttered to himself, then picked up his pace to catch up.

As he stepped up alongside her, Ava asked, "What did you say?"

"Let's shake things up," Eli said.

She narrowed her eyes, like she didn't think that was what she'd heard, but let it go. "Hopefully this will give us something new. I'm not even sure what I'm looking for."

"I'm not, either," Eli agreed. "But my gut agrees with yours. We missed something."

Her strides increased, and Eli kept pace, impressed with her speed. When they strode into the bar, the same bartender was there from earlier in the afternoon.

She frowned at the sight of them, but no one else in the bar—a pair of twenty-something guys deep in conversation and a woman in the corner who was staring vacantly at the wall—seemed to notice the filthy cops.

When they reached the counter, Ava leaned toward her, keeping her voice low. "I'm not sure if you know why we were in here earlier?"

"Looking for something to tell you where Jenny is hiding?" she guessed.

"Not exactly," Eli replied, surprised. He'd assumed she'd known about the bomb. "Do you know what happened with Jennilyn?"

She shrugged, picking at her faded nail polish. "The owner said something about a gas leak at her place? He was definitely lying, but Sasha took off before I could ask her about it."

"Is Jennilyn a friend of yours?" Ava asked.

"Yeah, kinda. I don't know her all that well really, but she sticks up for you if you need it."

"She stuck up for you before?" Eli asked, hoping this was the woman Jennilyn had helped by smashing a car.

Her gaze met his. Her eyes were slightly bloodshot, her eyelids drooping, but there was defiance there, too. "Yeah, she did. So whatever you're here for, whatever you think she did wrong, I'm not helping you."

Eli glanced at Ava, trying to silently communicate that she should take the lead. Hopefully the bartender would respond better to a woman.

"We're trying to help Jennilyn," Ava said, and the woman huffed.

"Really, we are," Ava said. "We're all part of the same community here. We need to look after each other."

Eli shot her a sideways glance, not wanting to distract her when her words were having an effect. The bartender's defensive posture was loosening, her angry gaze calming.

If only Ava's words were true. If only she planned to remain part of this community.

"What's your name?" Ava asked in the same soft, easygoing tone.

"Amber."

"Okay, Amber. So, I know Jennilyn went after some guy's car because he did something terrible to a friend of hers."

From the way Amber jerked at Ava's words, Eli didn't need to ask. Amber was the friend who'd been assaulted, who Jennilyn had tried to help.

"It's not the only time Jenny has tried to help out, right?" As Amber nodded slowly, Ava said, "I know she jumped into a bar fight, too, standing up for some women who were being harassed."

"She's always willing to put herself between other people and danger," Amber said softly. "I wish I were that brave."

Ava nodded. "Here's the thing, Amber. It's one thing to punch someone, to break a leg or smash a car. People recover from that. A bomb is something else, something that could destroy *Jennilyn's* future."

Amber jerked, dropping her hands to her sides as

she glanced wide-eyed from Ava to Eli and back again. "What bomb?"

"It wasn't a gas leak at her house," Ava said.

Amber's eyes got even wider and she jerked a hand up to her chest. "Someone *blew up* her house? Why? Because of what she did for me?"

"No, Amber. She blew up *her own* house," Ava said.

Amber was shaking her head before Ava finished. "No way."

"I know it seems strange, but it was her way of getting out of here. She set it off earlier than she planned," Eli said.

Amber looked like she was going to argue again, but Ava jumped in. "We were here earlier to see if she'd set a bomb at the bar, because we heard from her ex that she held a grudge against the owner. Because he didn't stand up against some of the wrongs Jennilyn had seen. Because she was tired of doing it herself."

Amber kept shaking her head, her overdyed red hair swishing across her face. "Her ex said that?" she scoffed. "Look, this place might not be Jenny's dream job." She waved a hand expansively, vaguely, at the room. "I mean, it's not exactly any of our dream jobs, right? But it pays okay. And she had *friends* here. Unlike Dennis, who nobody liked so he was always just hanging on to her friends. I mean, hell, he couldn't even hang on to a job. Even the Army kicked him out."

Eli felt a kick in his gut. "The Army kicked him out? I thought he and Jennilyn voluntarily left together? To start a new life in a small town?"

"Well, *she* left voluntarily. If he hadn't been kicked

out, she probably would have re-upped." Amber shrugged. "At least that's what she told me."

"Do you know where Jennilyn might be?" Ava asked, tension in her voice now, as she probably picked up on the same thing he was feeling.

Amber shrugged. "No. But she's not just tough. She's also smart. If her place was bombed, it wasn't Jenny blowing up her own house. It was someone else, maybe someone she beat up who couldn't take the humiliation. If it was that guy who attacked me…"

Amber swallowed hard enough for Eli to hear, then rushed on, "She's not hiding from the cops. She's hiding because someone is trying to kill her."

Eli held in a million curses, suddenly certain what had been nagging Ava that they'd missed.

It wasn't Jennilyn they needed to find. It was Dennis, who had completely played them.

Chapter Twenty-Six

"His name is Dennis Ryon?" Brady's voice echoed on speaker in the car.

They'd called him at home, after notifying the Chief. Brady had sounded tired when he picked up, but Ava had been impressed at how he'd instantly shifted into work mode when they updated him about what they'd learned.

"That's right," Eli confirmed. "We spoke to him about six hours ago at the Salmon Creek Motel. We're heading back there now. In the meantime, we're hoping you and Jason can dig up as much as possible."

"I'll give Jason a call and head into the station as soon as we get off the phone," Brady agreed.

"According to the bartender at Shaker Peak, Dennis was dishonorably discharged from the Army. That might be a place to start," Ava put in.

She gazed at Eli out of the corner of her eye as she spoke. His attention was fully on the road, both hands on the wheel, his expression intense. Fully focused on work again.

Another pang of regret struck and she tried to push it back, reminded herself she was doing the right thing.

She liked Eli too much to leap into something that had an expiration date.

Earlier tonight, she'd felt her first real stirrings of excitement about building a future in Jasper. In the past few days, things had finally started turning around. She was making progress with her coworkers. She'd accepted the strength and importance of her bond with Lacey, who was doing better each time Ava texted Marie or Tashya to check on her progress. And the possibility of a relationship with Eli had felt so *right*.

But Komi was her family. For five years, she'd done everything she could to mend that bond. If he was finally willing to repair it, she didn't want to be eighteen hundred miles away. She needed to be right there, needed him to see she was just as committed to being a family.

She missed Chicago. Missed her friends there, missed the buzz of the city and the easy comradery of her fellow officers in narcotics.

She would miss Jasper when she left, too. But she'd only been here for a few months. She couldn't trade the people she'd known all her life for what she'd barely started to build here.

Still, that ache in her chest didn't subside as she stared at Eli's profile. It had become so familiar in just a week. The idea of leaving him, of leaving the possibilities she felt when she looked at him, felt wrong, too.

"Ava. Ava, your phone is ringing."

She jerked, realizing she'd been so caught up in her own thoughts that Brady had already hung up.

"It might be Amber," Eli added, and she scrambled to pull the phone out of her pocket.

Before they'd left the bar, they'd tried to convince Amber to tell them where Jennilyn might be staying. She'd hesitated long enough that Ava suspected she knew, or at least had an idea. She'd steadfastly refused to give it up, only reluctantly agreeing to try and get a message to her.

"Hello?" Ava answered just before her phone would have gone to voice mail.

"Is this Officer Callan?"

The voice wasn't familiar and Ava's enthusiasm dimmed. "Speaking."

"This is Jennilyn Sanderson."

Eyes widening, Ava put her on speaker. "Jennilyn, thanks for contacting us."

Eli glanced at her, surprise on his face. But he stayed quiet.

"Yeah, well, Amber said you thought I blew up my own house."

"If you didn't do it, then who did?" Ava asked, keeping her tone even.

"Are you kidding me?" she snapped, then muttered, "And people wonder why I don't trust the cops to get things done."

"We came to your house because of something of yours we found near bomb materials," Ava told her, hoping she wasn't making a mistake. Since they'd spoken to Amber, that itchy feeling she'd had that something about their investigation was off track had disappeared. She was pretty sure she knew exactly who they were looking for, but she didn't want to lead Jennilyn. She wanted the woman to say it herself.

"That asshole," Jennilyn spat. "It figures. I dumped him and it's not enough to try and kill me. He also wants to frame me for my own death."

Eli's gaze darted to hers again and Ava nodded, knowing what he was thinking. Dennis hadn't been trying to frame Jennilyn for her own death—or at least, that hadn't been his primary objective. There had to be another target.

"You're talking about your ex, Dennis Ryon?" Ava asked, still in the same calm, neutral tone.

"Yeah, I'm talking about Dennis," Jennilyn snapped, then she blew out a loud breath. "Look, he's just… He's gotten scary. He's not the guy I thought I knew."

"Tell me what happened," Ava encouraged, hoping Jennilyn could give them insight into not just why Dennis was setting bombs, but who he might be targeting. Maybe she could even give them enough to get an arrest warrant. "How has he changed?"

"When I met him in the Army, he was so full of purpose. Then they accused him of misconduct. I don't know all of the details, but they claimed when he was overseas, he knocked down some civilians with his gun, kicked them, spat on them. He was pissed, said he was being railroaded because people didn't like him. He claimed the incident was blown out of proportion, that the civilians had posed a real threat and he'd only asked them to leave the area. He said some of his unit didn't like how he'd always be out in front, like he wanted the limelight, so when the civilians made the bogus charges, a couple of guys in the unit backed it. Which made sense to me. I always thought he was just confident, but yeah, it sometimes bordered on cocky. He didn't have tons of friends."

She sighed heavily. "Anyway, when the Army kicked him out, he asked me to go with him. We'd only been dating for a few months then, but I saw a future with him. I mean, I just *knew,* in this way I've never felt before, that we were supposed to be together."

Ava's gaze darted to Eli before she could stop herself. His gaze was locked on hers, projecting the same kind of understanding she felt. A bone-deep knowledge that she and Eli could have something special, the kind of gut feeling that almost never failed her in an investigation.

But gut feelings could be wrong. Jennilyn was proof of that, in more ways than one.

Eli broke eye contact first, his attention returning to the road as they traveled back the way they'd come early this afternoon, toward the motel where Dennis was staying. Hopefully, before they got there, either Jennilyn or their team would give them the ammunition they needed to bring him in.

"I understand," Ava said softly, this time keeping her gaze firmly on the phone as she felt Eli look her way again.

"I was wrong," Jennilyn said. "It took me a while to realize it, but after I agreed to go with him, we decided to move somewhere brand new. We checked all these places out, and from his perspective, none of them were good enough. Finally, I put my foot down in Jasper. This was it. I thought all we needed was a chance, a fresh start together, and we could make it work."

"What happened?" Ava pressed when she went silent.

"What *didn't* happen?" Bitterness underlaid each word. "He was getting into fights at Handall's Furniture, where he worked delivery. With his coworkers, with his boss. He hated the friends I was making here, thought they were bad-mouthing him and wanted me to stop hanging out with them—even though most of my friends I met at work. Plus, he was still *really* bitter about what had happened in the military, constantly talked about how it wasn't just a few bad apples who'd lied about him. It was the whole system out to screw him. He thought he should have still been in the Army, still working a job he actually loved. He started taking it out on me. I tried to be understanding, but it just kept getting worse, until finally I realized it wasn't everyone else making the problems. It was Dennis."

"So, you broke up with him," Ava said.

"Yeah. And he didn't take it well. He started screaming about how I was just like everyone else. Even put his fist through the wall. I'd never seen that side of him before."

"You were scared of him?"

"Hell, yes. Look, I'm no pushover. Dennis might be half a foot bigger than me and he might outweigh me by eighty pounds, but I got the same training he did. I don't show fear easily. Still, there was something in his eyes when I told him to move out…"

Ava started to ask about Dennis's training, but Jennilyn was talking again, faster now, the frustration and fear seeping further into her voice.

"I changed the locks, but he still found a way to

get in. He ripped up some of my clothes, smashed my computer."

"Did you contact the police?" Ava asked. They hadn't seen anything when they'd dug into Jennilyn's history, but they'd been focused on her as a suspect, not a target.

"No. I just—I didn't want to enrage him further. One of my friends has a camper, so I borrowed it, started staying out—well, somewhere Dennis wouldn't think to look. I figured it would blow over. Then I heard he got fired from his new job, too, and I knew that would set him off all over again. I started to think I was going to have to leave Jasper completely if I ever wanted to be free of him."

Ava felt Eli's gaze on her again, but she didn't need to glance over to know what he was thinking. A series of rejections over the past year, from the military to his girlfriend to multiple jobs. A pattern like that was always worrisome, especially when the person had a history of violence.

Although they hadn't checked if Dennis had a police record, given what Jennilyn was saying, Ava suspected the Army hadn't gotten it wrong when they'd kicked him out.

"Jennilyn, does Dennis have bomb training from the Army?"

There was a pause, and then Jennilyn admitted, "We both do. It's where I first met him, in bomb detection and disposal training."

Before Ava could ask for more details, Jennilyn rushed on, "But I swear, I've never *set* a bomb. Honestly,

I never even had a chance to detect or defuse one before Dennis got kicked out and I decided to go with him."

"What about Dennis?"

"I'm not sure. Look, I've been out of my place for a couple of weeks, ever since Dennis got in there and destroyed my things. I haven't been home since. I was still going to work, even though I knew it was a way for him to find me. I figured he'd show up there eventually. Stupidly, I thought he wouldn't want to make a scene in front of other people."

"He came to the bar?" Ava asked.

"No. I got a call from my neighbor saying my house blew up. I was on my way to work when he called and I turned right back around. Didn't call in or anything because I was so freaked out. I knew immediately it was Dennis. Right now, I'm just hiding, but he'll find me eventually if I stick around. So, I'm getting out of here before he figures out where I am."

"We can help you—" Ava started.

"No. I called because Amber said you thought *I* set that bomb. I'm not letting him destroy my reputation along with everything else. But if you think I'm trusting you to keep me safe, you haven't been listening. I know how this kind of thing always goes when men harass women."

"Blowing up a house is a lot more serious than harassment," Ava said.

"Yeah, well, maybe if you'd done something when he was harassing his coworkers, I wouldn't be in this position now!" There was a brief pause, then Jennilyn said, more calmly, "You want to deal with Dennis, great. Just don't expect me to do your work for you."

She hung up before Ava could ask anything else.

"I don't think Dennis wanted us to find those bomb materials at the JPG warehouse," Eli said.

It took Ava a minute to realize where he was going. "You think he was practicing, that he needed a place to keep the materials since he's been staying in a motel where a cleaning crew might come in. He wore gloves out of caution, not because he was expecting anyone to discover them. So, when we found the materials, he was worried it would lead us to him."

"Yeah. I think that's when he decided to hand us Jennilyn with the next set of materials. When he broke into her house, he didn't just destroy things. He also took her lighter. Something that would have her prints on it. It's why everything else was clean. Because this time, we *were* supposed to find it."

"We got lucky finding that," Ava disagreed.

"We did. I think we messed up his plan. I think he set it up, then planned to set off a bomb somewhere in town first and then call in a tip about the old sawmill."

Ava nodded slowly, the pieces falling into place. "Direct our investigation to Jennilyn and then blow her house when we went to talk to her. He was planning to make it look like she panicked after setting the bomb and took herself out."

"Right. Except we found the lighter too soon. He probably followed us to Jennilyn's house. Or maybe we arrived not long after he set the bomb there. Either way, *he* panicked when I saw him in the woods."

"Are you sure it was him?" Ava asked.

Eli laughed. "No. But it's my theory."

"It makes sense. You figure the original plan is that while we were digging through the evidence at the house, he'd be tracking down Jennilyn and killing her, then skipping town? Or maybe that he'd kill her first, leave her in the house so we'd find a body in the rubble?"

"It lines up with what she was saying about his escalating aggression," Eli said as he pulled off the road across the street from the motel, out of the line of sight from the rooms.

"It does," Ava said, troubled. "He could be going after everyone who he thinks did him wrong. It sounds like that's a long list. His colleagues, the military, Jennilyn's friends who didn't approve of him. If she's telling us the truth—and I think she is—he's a prime example of someone who blames others for his own failures, and is willing to take it out on everyone around him."

Eli glanced at his phone, silent in the console between them. "Brady said he'd text us as soon as he had anything, but I don't think we should wait."

"Yeah, I agree. If he's keeping tabs on things, he may know we were at the bar today talking to Jennilyn's friends. I'm sure he knows it was only a matter of time before his name came up. I want to get ahead of it. Maybe talk to him on the same pretense as before, more questions that are supposedly about Jennilyn, see if we can trip him up?"

"And hope that meanwhile Brady and Jason can get us enough for an arrest warrant?" Eli nodded. "Yeah.

If we don't get that, at least we can keep tabs on him, make sure he's not out planting any bombs."

"You ready?" Ava asked, reaching for the door handle.

"Let's do this," Eli said.

She followed him outside, across the street and as he carefully maneuvered around the bushes that had blocked their view from the rooms.

He took off running before she'd rounded the bushes, but she followed immediately, her pulse jumping and her hand hovering over her weapon.

Then she saw why he'd moved so quickly.

Dennis's room door was ajar, a man in a cleaning uniform standing outside of it.

He looked startled as they raced up to him, putting his hands in the air as Eli peered into the room and swore.

"Where is he?" Ava asked.

The man shook his head. "Don't know. He checked out an hour ago."

Chapter Twenty-Seven

Dennis Ryon was gone.

Ava and Eli had called it in immediately and every officer out on patrol was watching for him. Meanwhile, they'd returned to the police station to search for leads, and hopefully to get enough for an arrest warrant when they found him.

Ava stared at herself in the mirror in the ladies room, where she'd run to clean up as soon as they reached the station. Despite having rubbed her face and hands vigorously with paper towels to get off the dirt, her skin still had a strange grayish cast to it. There were dark circles under her eyes and a slump to her shoulders. She felt as exhausted as she looked, and it wasn't just from already having worked a full shift.

It was everything. A week ago, she'd been trying— and failing—to fit in with her colleagues, with her neighbors in Jasper. She'd felt lost, and lonely. Since then, Lacey had almost died and that moment had made her realize just how much she relied on her K-9 partner, at work and in her life. She'd made the first small step toward reconnecting with her brother. She'd finally started bonding with her coworkers. She'd met Eli.

An hour ago, when Komi had called, she'd been ready to toss everything she'd started building here, to run back to Chicago. As she stared at the locket around her neck—the one she'd worn for five years as a remembrance, a penance—she wondered if Chicago was really where she belonged.

She'd loved her career in the Chicago PD, loved working narcotics. But this week, she'd finally been finding her groove. The thrill of *this* job had started to fill her, the possibility of being a true community officer, the way she'd dreamed back when she was fifteen years old. The idea of leaving Lacey behind made panic build in her chest. Lacey wasn't just her partner—wasn't just the best partner she'd ever had—the dog was also her family.

She'd lost so much family already. She didn't want to do it again. If she left, would Lacey even understand that Ava couldn't bring her, that the K-9 technically belonged to the Jasper PD? Or would she feel as betrayed and devastated as Ava had felt when Komi had cut her out of his life?

Then, there was Eli. She'd only just met him, but he was more than a passing interest who would fade from her memory if she left Jasper and never came back. If she gave it time, she knew he would become someone important in her life. Would she find anyone like him in Chicago?

No, a voice whispered in her head. There was no one like Eli.

Still, how could she pass up a chance to make things right with Komi, the little brother who had felt like her shadow for most of her life? The little brother she'd missed so desperately for the past five years?

Scrubbing a hand across her eyes, Ava stared harder at her reflection, as if the answer were there in her gaze. All she saw was someone who looked slightly panicked, someone with no answers. Not for her life and not in this case.

"Get it together," she whispered. Now wasn't the time to make big life decisions. Right now, she needed to do her job and stop Dennis Ryon from setting a bomb.

Tossing the dirty paper towel in the trash and squaring her shoulders, she headed back to the conference room.

While she'd been cleaning up, Brady and Jason had arrived. Both officers looked tired. Brady's always closely groomed beard seemed like it had grown in the past few hours, and Jason kept rubbing the back of his hand over his eyes.

Eli had taken the time to clean up, too. He'd done a better job of it than she had, somehow getting not only his skin clean, but also his uniform. He even looked energized, his bright blue eyes intense as his gaze met and held hers just long enough to feel intimate, but not long enough to draw attention.

Ava flushed, too many visions of Eli flashing through her mind. When she'd first met him, ultra-focused on his bomb-detection robot. On the case together, scouting out behind the warehouses. At Rose Café, all his attention on her, as if she were the most important thing in the world. At Jennilyn's house, in those seconds before the house blew and she knew he was in danger. Earlier tonight, disappointed understanding flashing on his face when she shifted from date mode into all work.

As Eli gave Brady and Jason the longer version of what he'd told them over the phone about Dennis, Ava let herself imagine him in the future. His hands brushing hers quickly while they were on the job, a shared, secret glance. Melding her lips to his again, feeling that same sense of inevitability. Even further, into territory she'd never daydreamed about with anyone else: meeting his family, looking for a house with him. Something permanent, somewhere between Jasper and McCall.

She blinked the images away before they could continue, focusing on Eli's words.

"Let's split up the work. Since Dennis doesn't have a police record, Ava and I will focus on digging into his history. We'll see if we can contact Jennilyn again, check out his social media. Try to figure out who else he's close to or where he might be hiding. Brady and Jason, I want you two to focus on his next target. If we can't find him first, we need to get in front of a bomb."

"Sounds good," Jason said.

"Yeah, I'm worried that he took off," Brady added. "Either he did it as a precaution because you found him to ask about Jennilyn or he knows you're on to him. Whatever the case, right now, we've got three options. He's gone to ground somewhere to plan. He's skipped town already and given up on revenge for now. Or he's moved up his timetable, whatever it was, and we probably don't have long before there's another bomb."

"Agreed," Eli said. "I doubt he skipped town. I'm

hoping he's gone to ground, found himself another hiding place, maybe with a friend we don't know about or at a campsite. Otherwise, we probably have a day or even hours until he sets off another bomb."

ELI SQUEEZED A hand around the back of his neck, trying to ease the tension from too many hours on a laptop. So far, what he'd found was unsurprising and unhelpful.

Dennis Ryon was a loner. His social media presence was almost nonexistent. He had an account with no profile picture. A few people had tagged him over the years, from Army buddies to coworkers. Even in those photos, he was on the edges, slightly separated from everyone, the look in his eyes disinterested.

Eli and Ava had reached out to Jennilyn again, but she'd had little to say on the friend front. They'd slowly faded away, she'd told them, until she couldn't really say if he'd stayed in touch with any friends.

Targets were the opposite. There were too many to check out individually, too much wasted time. Colleagues from the military—two of whom actually lived on the outskirts of Jasper—or from the job he'd had at Handall's Furniture just inside the Jasper town limits, or from Blaze's River Tours and Rafting, where he'd told Jennilyn he was finally going to start fresh. His attempt to prove to her that he was going to change. He'd been fired even before they opened, not long after she'd broken up with him. Then there were Jennilyn's friends at the bar, people he thought had a hand in convincing Jennilyn to instigate the breakup.

They'd kept the small department updated anyway,

made sure officers out on the streets drove by potential targets in case anything looked suspicious. Or they got lucky and spotted Dennis. So far, that hadn't yielded any results, either.

"It's six a.m.," Brady announced.

Eli blinked at him, refocusing. Had they really been in this conference room all night?

"I've got to get some coffee, something to eat," Brady added. "Or I'm going to crash soon."

"Millard's Diner opens at six," Jason put in. "I'll go over with you and grab some food." He glanced at Eli and Ava. "You two want anything?"

"Coffee," they said in unison, drawing Eli's attention back to her.

She looked tired, but there was a determination in her light brown eyes. Curls had slid free from her bun hours ago and she'd been tucking them absently behind her ears ever since. Two of them had bounced loose again and Eli longed to pull the rest of her hair free.

Shaking off the thought, he added, "Food would be great, too. Anything with protein. I think I've exhausted the information we can find from the station. We need to get out on the streets soon."

"Same for me on the food," Ava said. "Thanks," she added as Jason and Brady hurried out of the room.

When she stood and dialed a number on her cell phone, Eli stood, too. Instead of stretching like he'd planned, he found his feet moving toward her until he was standing close enough to run his hand through the curls dangling across her cheek.

"Hi, Marie? I was just calling to check... She will?"

A smile burst on her face and her gaze lifted to his, happiness overriding the exhaustion. "Okay... Okay. Thank you!"

When she hung up, she told him, "Lacey is doing great. I'll be able to take her home tomorrow afternoon."

"That's great," he said, imagining how happy the German shepherd would be to see Ava, and vice versa.

Leaning backward, he peered into the bullpen through the part of the conference room that was glassed in. The bullpen was empty, most of the other officers out on the street, watching for anything of concern or any sign of Dennis.

Refocusing his attention on Ava, he said softly, "Whatever you decide to do after this case is finished, I'll support you."

Surprise flashed in her gaze, followed by an uncertainty that told him he still had a chance.

Trying to taper the hope that flared, he stepped slightly closer and added, "But I have to at least make sure you know how much I want you to stay."

She blinked, and this close, he could see the desire overtaking her uncertainty.

Before she could regain her equilibrium, he reached up and tucked that curl behind her ear, letting his hand slide over her soft skin. Her eyes dilated and she swayed toward him just slightly.

It was a bad idea to kiss her in a police station. But his mind couldn't override his emotions as he leaned in and pressed his lips against hers. Softly, enjoying the plumpness of her lips, the way her eyes slid shut and her palms planted against his chest like she needed him to support her.

His thumb stroked the edge of her cheek as his fingers twitched in her hair, anxious to pull the rest of it free. His lips moved gently over hers, enjoying, savoring, memorizing.

She sighed, her lips parting, and he couldn't resist slipping his tongue into her mouth, using his free hand to pull her tight against him.

Her hands spasmed against his chest, then fisted there, like she wasn't sure if she wanted to push him away or yank him closer still.

A noise in the bullpen made her pull back, her gaze unfocused.

He glanced behind him, but there was no one. He breathed her in once more—the faint, intoxicating scent of cocoa butter he'd started to crave whenever she wasn't around. Then he forced himself to step away from her, not to tarnish her reputation in the station where he wanted her to remain.

Ava, stay, clogged in his throat, and he forced himself not to say it, not to pressure her when he knew how badly she missed Chicago, missed her brother.

"I…" Ava laughed, high and nervous, her hands tucking curls back into that bun. "I shouldn't have done that. We need to focus on work."

He smiled at her, remembering the last time she'd kissed him and then told him they needed to keep things professional. Remembering the promise he'd made to pursue her as soon as this case was over.

"I think this time, the blame is on me," he teased

her. "But anytime you feel like instigating something, I'll be good with it."

He grinned, and she blinked at him a few times, then her own grin emerged.

The grin slowly faded, her gaze turning pensive. But there was something in her eyes that made his heart leap. "I think—"

Her words were cut off as Brady and Jason rushed into the room, no take-out bags in sight.

"There was a line at Millard's Diner today," Jason said, breathless. "People who'd driven into town early for events."

"There's a military veterans event scheduled to start in a few hours at Bartwell Brewing Company. Today is also the grand opening of Blaze's River Tours and Rafting."

As Ava swore softly, Eli said, "This is it. It's got to be one of those events. We just found Dennis's target."

Chapter Twenty-Eight

"Which one is it?" Jason asked, glancing from Eli to Brady to Ava and back again. "Bartwell Brewing Company or Blaze's River Tours and Rafting? The military that started Dennis's downward trajectory or the company that fired him most recently, ruining his shot to turn things around?"

Eli's pulse picked up, anxiety spiking at the idea of searching the wrong place. "Jennilyn said the military was his dream job. This veterans event isn't specifically connected to anyone who he thinks turned him in and got him kicked out, but he blames the whole military now. Blaze's was a much newer job, not as prized, but the specific person who fired him will probably be at the event." Eli shrugged. "I could see Dennis picking either one."

"When do the events start?" Ava asked.

Eli glanced at her, trying not to think about what she might have been getting ready to say before Jason and Brady burst into the room. She'd looked so serious, but not like she was about to shoot him down. Instead, she'd seemed as though she might have been ready to give him hope, to say that her mind wasn't made up about returning to Chicago. If that were the case, would he be so wrong to do his best to convince her to stay?

He shook the thoughts free, focusing on what mattered right now, as Ava continued speaking.

"If he's targeting an event, especially now when he's truly gone into hiding, he's probably not just aiming at a few specific people who did him wrong. He's looking to make a statement, either to the military or to this town."

The grim prediction made the room go silent briefly, then Jason spoke up.

"The military event starts at nine, but according to a couple of Army guys who were picking up coffee, there's already a line. Blaze's grand opening starts at eight, but it sounds like there's a line there, too, because they're giving away gift certificates for rafting adventures. The first fifty people get extra raffle tickets."

Ava glanced at her phone. "It's six twenty now. Not a lot of time to do a thorough search of each of those buildings, plus any outdoor setups."

"Not to mention defuse anything we find," Eli said. "Especially since we can't rule out that Dennis might have picked *both* events. If there are two bombs, it's not like I can be in two places at once."

Brady swore. "Divide and conquer? Jason and I can search Bartwell Brewing, since the military event starts a little later. You and Ava go to Blaze's. If we find something at Bartwell before you're finished searching, we can get someone to take over for you. We can ask the Chief to put everyone on standby to evacuate either place if we find anything. If we're not finished searching, I think we should just clear out both spots at seven thirty."

Eli nodded, waving frantically at the Chief, who chose that moment to walk by the conference room.

He did a quick turn, rushing inside, his craggy face serious, his hazel eyes intense. "What's happening?"

"We think we know what Dennis is going to target," Eli said. He told the Chief their plan.

The Chief glanced at Ava. "I wish we had Lacey right now."

"Me, too," Ava said. "But she's not cleared—"

"No," the Chief cut her off. "I'm not suggesting you bring her in while she's still healing. She's an officer, too. I'm not risking the rest of her career for one investigation, no matter how important. Besides, if she's not fully healed, she might not be up for the job. The plan we have is good. I trust you all to do what needs to be done." He glanced at his watch. "But you have one hour. Then we're evacuating those buildings, plus anything nearby. If a bomb goes off downtown, especially something like the one at Sanderson's house…"

"There could be a lot of casualties," Eli said, feeling the pressure build. On a Saturday morning, even people who had no interest in either of the big events would be downtown, enjoying the warming weather.

"I'll be in command mode," Chief Walters said. "Radio if you need anything."

As they hurried for the door, the Chief called after them, "Good luck."

Eli raced for his SUV, the adrenaline rush chasing away the last of his fatigue. Mentally, he catalogued all of the gear in the back of his vehicle, deciding he'd go in with just his standard kit of bomb disposal tools, plus his portable X-ray scanner. Easy to carry and he'd maneuver a lot faster than the robot, especially with a lot of people around. He didn't want to panic anyone.

He waved to Brady and Jason as the pair got into Brady's police vehicle and headed to Bartwell's, lights and sirens off to keep everyone calm. It wasn't a long drive to the brewery, located in an alley off Third Street.

Blaze's was even closer, on Main Street just like the station. With Ava right behind him, Eli hopped into his SUV and turned out of the station, onto the street.

He couldn't help but notice how many people were already out, walking their dogs or pushing strollers and laughing, carefree. Enjoying the first weekend of the year that was supposed to reach almost seventy degrees.

"Why couldn't we have gotten lucky with some thunderstorms," Eli muttered.

"We'll get there in time," Ava said, her voice confident. "He's not going to blow this bomb until the event is underway. Whatever he's targeting, he wants to be remembered for this explosion."

Eli nodded, but he couldn't help but picture the blast of heat and sound that had lifted him off his feet at Jennilyn's house. An explosion triggered by Dennis at their arrival.

"We need to act normal, pretend we're not in a rush," Eli said as he parked across the street from Blaze's, which was bursting with people.

The line was already snaking down the street, people laughing and chatting, kids snacking on bags of popcorn the company was handing out. Employees milled around, handing out flyers and pointing to a fancy kayak on display in front of the store. A grand prize for one lucky raffle winner, according to the sign.

Eli texted Brady the same thing as he told Ava, "Try not to draw attention. Maybe even ask a few people about Jennilyn when we arrive."

Ava's brown eyes were wary as she stared back at him. "You're worried that if he spots us—"

"He could set the bomb off early."

Chapter Twenty-Nine

Eli pasted a smile on his face as he slung his plain black nylon bag over his shoulder. It could pass as a laptop case, but it actually contained bomb disposal tools. Everything from a hook-and-line kit to a multi-tool with knives and plyers to carabiners, mirrors and a compass. All the things he'd need to defuse a bomb if they found a live one. Just not a bomb suit to keep himself safe, because right now, it was more important not to incite panic or cause Dennis to set the bomb off early.

He glanced at Ava, who'd looked worried when he'd told her he was leaving his suit and the robot in the vehicle. He gave her a confident nod, hoping she couldn't tell that he was nervous.

Usually, he arrived at the site of a potential bomb with cautious anxiety, trusting his training and his equipment. Usually, beneath the worry over what he might find was an undercurrent of excitement. The knowledge that he could defuse and dismantle whatever he came across. The pride in taking care of his community.

Today, that excitement was totally missing, replaced by a churning in his gut. His instincts, telling him they were going to run into trouble? Or concern for Ava, who would be going into a building right alongside him that might be set to blow?

It was a little bit of both, he realized, as she gave him a similar nod in return, like she was also trying to put on a brave front for him.

Striding through the crowds, Eli scanned the outside area for anywhere a bomb might be hidden. The kayak on display was the most obvious option. As Ava chatted with a few people in line, asking with casual interest if they knew Jennilyn Sanderson and if anyone had seen her recently, Eli pretended to tie his shoe next to the kayak.

As he bent down, he peered beneath the kayak and along the metal display holding it up, looking for any sign of a bomb. There was nothing. With a quick tug to the knot on his shoe, he stood and said to Ava in a tone meant to be overheard, "Let's step inside and see if anyone there has seen Jennilyn."

She nodded, thanking the people she'd been chatting with, and followed him as he asked the employee holding the door to let them inside.

The minute he stepped inside, a weight pressed on Eli's chest. The store was probably a thousand square feet. It was packed with rafting and camping gear, each shelf a potential hiding spot for a bomb. That wasn't including the office or storage areas Eli couldn't see. There was no way to inspect it all in less than an hour.

There were no customers allowed inside yet, but half a dozen employees hurried through the room, straightening merchandise and setting out flyers advertising the company's Salmon River tours on every available surface.

Eli glanced around the room, trying to decide what would be Dennis's best bet if he wanted a bomb to remain unseen during a busy opening. Dropping to the ground, he pulled a mirror from his kit and started peering underneath shelves and counters.

"What's he doing?" one of the employees asked.

"Safety check. We're making sure nothing is unstable," Ava told her loudly, then asked Eli, "How can I help?"

A couple of other employees gave them perplexed looks, but continued working.

Eli handed her a mirror. "Help me search."

Half an hour later, his body aching from jumping up and down, he hurried over to Ava. "Find anything?"

She shook her head.

Swearing under his breath, Eli snagged one of the closest employees and asked, "Where's the owner?"

The frazzled-looking woman pointed vaguely toward the front of the store, where a man had just entered. Then she pulled free, continuing to set out flyers.

Eli followed Ava, not bothering to act so casual now that they were inside, out of sight from prying eyes. Wherever Dennis was, it wasn't in the store.

"Are you the owner?" Ava asked when they reached a tall stocky white man with prematurely gray hair and an infectious smile.

"That's me," he replied, his smile fading in the face of their serious expressions. "Blaze Peterson. What can I do for you? If this is about the crowds, we'll be keeping a count on how many people enter at once. We know the fire code."

"That's not it," Eli said, keeping his voice low. "Have you seen Dennis Ryon recently?"

"Dennis?" Blaze scowled. "I had to fire him a few weeks ago. I thought he was going to be great with stocking inventory, considering what a strong-looking guy he is, and being former Army and all. But he was always picking fights with my other employees, acting like he was in charge when he wasn't."

"Is there any chance he still has access to your store?" Eli pressed.

Blaze scowled. "I'd like to say no. I never gave him a key. He wasn't senior enough for that. But I overheard him bragging to one of our other employees that his work in the Army had taught him to get in anywhere and that our locks were a joke."

"Do you have any reason to think he's been in the store recently?" Ava asked.

Blaze shifted his weight, starting to look nervous. "Why?"

"We think he may be targeting someone for what he considers revenge. We're just not sure who that might be."

Blaze's meaty hands formed fists. "Well, I can tell you that he threatened to destroy me when I fired him. The look on his face when he said it made me nervous, I have to admit. Do you think he's planning to ruin our grand opening?"

"It's our goal to stop that," Ava said. "What area would Dennis be most familiar with? Is there somewhere he spent a lot of time working or during breaks?"

Eli nodded at her, liking the way she was thinking. There was no way to search the entire store before their seven-thirty deadline. Most likely, they'd need to call the Chief and evacuate, which meant a potential risk that Dennis could set off a bomb during that evacuation. By starting somewhere Dennis felt comfortable, maybe they'd get lucky.

"Yeah, sure," Blaze said. "He was going to be a tour guide once we opened. He was a strong kayaker and we were working to get him familiar with the script and the river. Until then, he was helping us with stock. It's not the best layout for big stock, but we wanted as much space as possible for the actual store. So, we kept our stock in the basement."

Blaze pointed to a door marked Employees Only and Eli hurried toward it, Ava on his heels. If you wanted to cause structural damage to take down a whole building, a basement was a good location to set a bomb. Not to mention that he'd chosen that spot when he'd blown up Jennilyn's house.

"There's an outside entrance, too," Blaze called after them, and the sudden urgency in his voice made Eli glance back. "A service elevator that goes to the back. In case we want to haul boats out that way. I know I locked it when I closed up last night, but I found it unlocked this morning when I showed up at six."

Sharing a worried glance with Ava, Eli pulled open the door to the basement and his pulse ratcheted up more. The stairs were dimly lit and his footsteps echoed as he raced down the extra-wide staircase. At the bottom, he found another light switch and flipped it.

Hopeful anxiety shifted into defeat as he took in the space, which looked as large as the store's footprint above. Big metal shelves took up a lot of the space. Huge boxes labeled with pictures of kayaks and canoes were stacked on the bigger bottom shelves and smaller boxes with other camping gear was up higher. Open stock—or maybe employee kayaks and oars for the tours—were lined up to the right of the staircase. Excess streamers and a Grand Opening sign half the size of the one out front were stacked on top of the boats.

Eli cursed, staring into the cavernous space. It would be easy to place a bomb anywhere down here. It would take forever to clear.

He looked at Ava, ready to split up the space and start working, get as far as possible, when a scurrying sound toward the back of the basement made him freeze.

Just an animal? Or the shuffle of someone's shoe as they tried to hide?

Dropping his hand to his weapon, Eli gestured for Ava to move down the aisle in front of them while he went down the next one.

Eli moved quickly, cursing the way Blaze had built the shelving, so each of the aisles had a break partway down them. New aisles started up again in a staggered design, so he could only see halfway to the back of the basement.

Hurrying down the section he could see, hearing Ava's lighter tread in the aisle beside him, Eli pulled up short in the open space that bisected the aisles. He glanced in both directions, seeing no one, and was about to shift into the aisle to his right that would take him to the back of the space, when he spotted a plain black box the size of a suitcase that didn't look like anything around it.

Awareness from all of his training screamed at him.

Pivoting back, he knelt down and peered between two boxes. His heart gave an extra thump as he looked closer. The plastic container had no labels. It definitely didn't belong.

Setting down his tool kit, he checked for any obvious trip wires on the outside of the case. When he saw none, he pulled out his handheld X-ray machine.

"Is that what I think it is?" Ava asked in a whisper, nerves in her voice as she settled on her heels beside him.

"We're about to find out." He turned on the machine and swore at what it revealed. "It's a bomb." He peered closer, inspecting it for any sign that opening the case would set it off. When he was sure it wouldn't, he slowly opened the lid, double-checking with his mirror to be sure there wasn't a trigger he'd missed.

With the lid open, Ava gasped. "This is no pipe bomb."

"No." It was an IED packed with enough explosives to potentially take down the building. "This is probably what he used at Jennilyn's house." Eli glanced around the basement, searching for an obvious ignition source, but saw none. Maybe Dennis leaving the bomb next to a boiler at Jennilyn's had been unintentional. Just an easy spot to hide it.

That didn't mean a bomb of this size, placed below the building, couldn't cause enough structural damage to bring it down. It probably would. But it was unlikely to cause quite the fireball they'd seen at Jennilyn's.

A small hint of relief filled him and it grew when he looked closer at the bomb. "There's a timer, but it's not activated. We'll get the robot in here and get it contained."

He checked it over more carefully, making sure he wasn't missing anything, as he told Ava, "Check in with Brady and Jason, will you? Make sure we're only dealing with one bomb. Then let's try to get the robot down here discreetly, maybe from the back entrance. If Dennis is watching, he could activate this remotely. Normally, I'd evacuate now, but I think that will set him off, especially if this is the only bomb. Makes it more likely he's nearby, watching."

"On it," she replied, pulling out her phone and tapping away.

Almost immediately, she was tucking her phone back into her pocket. "They're pretty sure Bartwell's is clear. They're going to double-check everything, but one of the veterans had actually worked in bomb disposal for the military for more than a decade. He helped them check it."

"That's lucky," Eli said, his tension slipping down another notch. But the fact that there was only one bomb made it even more important not to let Dennis know they'd found this one. "Now, let's radio in to the Chief what we found. Ideally, I'll get this disarmed quietly and no one outside the department will even know there was a threat. Still, I want the team on standby to evacuate in case I run into trouble."

Ava nodded, giving him a reassuring smile. "You've got this."

He smiled back, knowing she was right. No bomb dismantling was a guarantee, but he knew he could do this safely.

Picking up his mirror again, he was leaning toward the bomb when a gunshot rang out, hitting a box one shelf over. The side of the box popped open and a waterfall of colorful folding knives spilled to the floor beside them.

Eli spun toward the back of the basement, where the shot had come from, and swore as a figure darted out of sight. Then another gunshot rang out.

This one hit closer, and Eli tackled Ava, pushing her into the aisle she'd walked down. As a third gunshot bounced off the metal shelf above the bomb, Eli cringed.

Then, a sound even worse reached his ears. A set of beeps from where he'd just been working.

They were pinned down. And the bomb had just been activated.

Chapter Thirty

Eli was squashing her beneath him, pressing her against the shelving as he tried to shield her from the gunshots.

When a series of beeps sounded beside her and Ava spotted a red light from between the shelves, she swore. "Is that what I think it was?"

Eli's voice, calm and confident even in the most stressful situations, was tense. "He activated the bomb."

"Can you defuse it from here?" Ava shifted beneath Eli, trying to pull him with her closer to the shelving unit, closer to the bomb. Away from the bullets.

He was more solid than he looked, and even though he let her move them against the shelf, he wouldn't let her slip out from underneath him.

She couldn't tell where Dennis was, but judging by where the gunshots had hit, he could probably still see them. The fact that he hadn't hit them didn't mean he was a bad shot. It meant he was a sadistic bastard who wanted to pin them down, make them watch the count-down.

Since he knew exactly when it was set to blow, he could keep them pinned long enough to prevent them from defusing the bomb. He could give himself just enough time to get out, and watch them get buried in the rubble.

"Can you defuse it?" Ava asked again, when Eli didn't respond. She twisted beneath him, trying to get a better look at what was happening. They were facing the wrong direction and it was awkward.

"No. I can probably reach it from here, but I'd have to move it toward me to work on it, and I don't know if that would set it off. I didn't have enough time to inspect it for anti-handling devices. Plus, my tools are out in the aisle and I can't get to those. Dammit!" he swore as another gunshot blasted, sending a waterfall of ropes on top of them.

"Do you see him?"

"No." Eli shoved some of the rope off them. Then he twisted, managing to keep himself on top of her while turning to face the direction where Dennis had to be hiding. "I think he's hiding on one of the bottom shelves. They're a little emptier on the back half of the shelves, from what I can tell. But I think he's close. He's using a kayak box as cover and peering over it to shoot. It puts him slightly above us, gives him some cover."

"Is he trying to shoot the bomb?"

"No. He's trying to stop us from disarming it."

"If you move a little, I can help aim at him," Ava whispered, hesitant to squirm out from underneath him while he was aiming his weapon in Dennis's direction. She didn't want to throw him off if he got a shot.

"We have to be careful. If we just injure him, he'll be able to use his remote detonator. If we get a shot, it has to be a kill shot. I'll keep my weapon on him. You call it in to the Chief," Eli insisted. "We need to get officers in from the other direction. They can enter through that other doorway. Blaze must not have realized Dennis was still here when he found it unlocked."

"If we trap him, he won't have anything to lose. He'll just set off the bomb!"

"What choice do we have? We need to evacuate as many people as we can."

He didn't say it, but she knew what he was thinking from the hard set to his voice. He thought she should be one of those people. He thought he could keep Dennis from shooting her while she ran back the way they'd come. Leaving him behind to die in the rubble with Dennis.

Panic fluttered in her chest, even though she'd never leave Eli alone. There had to be a better plan, a way to get to Dennis without him detonating the bomb.

Ava maneuvered awkwardly, digging her phone out of her pocket. Not wanting her voice to carry, she texted the Chief instead, giving him an update but warning him not to breach. Not yet.

She glanced at the time on her phone and her pulse skipped. Ten minutes until they'd originally planned to evacuate. It would probably be far less before police arrived and started clearing people from the store and the sidewalk above them.

The police would try to do it as calmly and quietly as possible, but with that many people, it wouldn't be silent. Dennis would probably hear the evacuation, especially once they started clearing everyone from inside the store.

Once that happened, it didn't matter what the countdown on the timer read. Dennis would just use his remote detonator and blow up as many people as he could.

The Chief responded to her text immediately, exactly how she expected. He was sending all available officers to evacuate the store and the surrounding area and he'd put help on standby. Ava set the phone on the floor beside her and squeezed her eyes shut, saying a silent prayer. The station was only a few minutes away. She needed to move fast.

Squirming quickly out from underneath Eli, Ava pivoted. Instead of pushing herself up beside him, she slid in the other direction.

"What are you doing?" Eli whispered.

"I'm going to need you to distract him in a minute."

"Ava, *no.*"

"This is our other choice, Eli. I'm not letting you sacrifice yourself for the rest of us." Checking to be sure she wouldn't accidently knock anything into the bomb, Ava slid a box labeled Flashlights into the aisle.

It was heavier than she'd expected and made a soft *thump* as it landed on the floor.

Silently, she swore, but Eli shoved one of the thicker, heavier ropes against the shelf across the aisle, making more noise. Then he fired a single bullet.

The shot echoed as it hit metal and Ava hoped the noise would cover the sound of her sliding onto the shelf where the box had been. She pulled herself across it with her arms, trying to be as silent as possible. A sharp edge of the metal shelf snagged her pant leg, piercing the skin beneath, and she clamped down on her jaw to keep from shrieking at the sudden, surprising pain.

Reaching back, she freed the material. Blood slicked her hand, more than she'd expected, and she swiped it against her pant leg. There was no time to worry about whether she'd hurt herself badly. Not when she needed all of her focus to find and sneak up on Dennis.

Her heart thundered in her ears as she slid out onto the aisle on the other side. Pulling herself into a crouch, Ava took her pistol out of its holster, trying to stay as small as possible against the shelf.

Since the aisles were staggered, even if Dennis peered out through the aisle on the other side, he shouldn't be able to see her. Not yet. Hopefully he'd just assume she'd slid backward in the same aisle as Eli, out of sight. But once she moved into the bisecting aisle, she'd be out in the open. A target for Dennis, but also a warning to him of what she planned. A chance for him to set off the bomb with a single press of his finger.

She should have taken more time to formulate a plan, to decide on a signal with Eli. Instead, she'd acted on instinct, knowing time was limited.

Staying close to the shelving, Ava stood slowly and moved on soft feet toward the front of the aisle. She wanted to look down at the bomb, to see how much time they had left, but she forced her gaze to stay focused. It didn't matter what the timer read.

Painfully slowly, she eased her head forward just enough to peer around the shelf. Her heart thumped hard when she spotted the kayak box on the bottom shelf across the aisle and over one. The spiky tops of

Dennis's blondish-brown hair were just visible above the box.

He was only eight feet away from her. But eight feet was too far when it meant sprinting toward him and tackling him in a way that didn't allow him to detonate the bomb. Especially when she had no idea whether the device he was using to control it was buried in his pocket or clutched in his free hand.

There had to be a way. Ava glanced around, moving only her eyes, not wanting to make any movements that Dennis might spot.

Her breath stuttered in her throat as his hand—holding a cell phone—appeared at the edge of the box, clutching it as if for stability. Then the top of his head and his gun popped up quickly above the box and he fired a single shot toward Eli.

Ava's hand jerked, instinct wanting to take over. Wanting to fire back and protect her partner.

Except Dennis wasn't trying to hit Eli. He just wanted to keep him pinned. Since no bullets had been fired at her, he hadn't realized she'd moved.

She could do this.

One of Dennis's hands was holding his gun. The other was still clutching the edge of the box. His phone was pressed between his hand and the box. It had to be how he was controlling the bomb.

Ava squeezed her eyes shut, focusing on evening out her breathing. She was a good shot. But it wasn't a big target. And she'd only get one chance.

Opening her eyes, Ava glanced down, making sure her leg wasn't dripping enough blood to make her slip.

She cringed at the small puddle at her feet, then moved that leg slightly forward, away from it. There was no room for error.

Lifting her weapon slowly, Ava eased it past the edge of the shelf, lining her eye up with it. She took one last breath, then exhaled as she pulled the trigger.

A scream echoed with the gunshot, but Ava didn't wait to see if she'd hit her target. She just shoved her gun back in its holster and launched herself away from the aisle.

Before she reached the shelving where Dennis was hiding, three more gunshots rang out from behind her. Eli, knowing exactly what distraction she needed.

Pushing off when she was halfway into the aisle, Ava crashed into Dennis, slamming both of them through the shelving and into the aisle on the other side.

Her head and back skimmed the top of the shelf above them. Pain erupted all over her body, but Ava ignored it, her gaze going to Dennis's hand that had held the cell phone. It was covered in blood. And it was empty. She'd hit her target.

Her relief was short-lived as he flipped beneath her, powerful enough to send her to the ground. He smashed a huge fist into her bicep and she slid across the floor, back into the shelving. A box fell from above, slamming into her and stealing her breath.

He scrambled the other way, toward the gun he'd dropped.

Then another gunshot rang out, making Dennis scurry backward as Eli raced toward them, his gun centered on Dennis. "Don't move!"

Ava shoved the box off her, trying to catch her breath. Pulling her weapon from her holster with a hand that trembled, she aimed it at Dennis.

He was crouched on the ground, his gaze darting to her left.

Ava's gaze followed, landing on his cell phone just as he made a leap for it.

She wasn't sure who fired first, her or Eli.

Dennis dropped instantly. She didn't need to check to know he was dead.

Head and leg throbbing, lungs aching with each breath, her gaze rose to Eli. She tried to shut out the pain, to ignore the relief that he was okay and focus on what mattered most right now. "How much time do we have?"

Eli holstered his weapon and spun back toward the bomb.

His curse reached her just as she raced up next to him. "He wasn't waiting for the grand opening to start."

She stared at the bright red numbers on the bomb.

They had less than a minute until it exploded.

Chapter Thirty-One

"Get out of here *now*," Eli said, dropping to the ground next to the bomb.

If only he had his robot. With its disruption tools that could separate a bomb from its trigger without setting it off. Or his bomb suit, to protect himself in case anything went wrong.

Of course, even a bomb suit, while it could protect him from bomb fragments, could only do so much when it came to the overwhelming force of an IED like this. It didn't matter how protected he was from the initial blast if it brought the building crashing down on top of him.

Right now, he'd even settle for his containment chamber. With an IED of this size, with this type of explosives, it wouldn't contain the whole blast. But it would be blunted enough that it wouldn't take down the building. Most likely, it would blunt it enough to save the lives of everyone here, especially if he could set the bomb inside the chamber and run.

There were so many options for dismantling a bomb like this. Far, far at the bottom of that list was what he was doing now, tackling it with his most basic tools, no protection and barely any time.

One wrong move and it wouldn't just be his own life gone. It would be everyone in the immediate vicinity. Beyond that, there would be amputations from the blast and flying debris, contusions and overpressure injuries that ended up being fatal after someone thought they'd survived the worst of it.

But he had no other option. The timer was already down to forty-nine seconds.

When Ava didn't move, he wasted precious seconds to look up at her, to take in the panicked expression in her eyes. Vowing to get through this, to have a chance to fight for her, he snapped, "Go now, Ava. Help them evacuate."

Instead, she dropped to her knees beside him. Her voice was calm and sure. "Tell me how to help."

Swearing, he stared at the bomb, assessing as fast as he could, thinking back to the pieces of devices they'd found at the warehouse and the sawmill. To the very limited information forensics had gathered so far from the bomb set in Jennilyn's basement. Clues to Dennis's methods? Or a way to lead them off track?

All the materials they'd found intact at the warehouse and sawmill had been pieces of pipe bombs. They'd been nothing like the higher explosive load at Jennilyn's house, a bomb they only had small pieces of to analyze. Nothing like the more sophisticated IED staring back at him now. Enough explosive material to take down a building, and the potential for hidden anti-tampering devices that would set it off if he attempted the wrong approach.

He started to tell Ava to radio the Chief, but she was

already doing it, advising him to evacuate now, to do it loudly and quickly.

Almost instantly, he heard Arthur Rutledge's voice booming over a loudspeaker, asking everyone to leave the area as quickly as possible.

Eli tuned out the details he knew would follow: leaving behind possessions. Leaving in an orderly fashion. Helping anyone who needed assistance, but moving fast. *Moving fast.*

If there was any chance that they could all evacuate far enough, he would have grabbed Ava and run, too. Left the area and let the building blow. Prioritizing life over property. But he only had thirty-six seconds left.

The people outside in line had a chance to get clear of the explosive range if they ran. With a bomb this size, ideally they would get at least fifty feet away from the bomb. That would probably save their lives from the initial blast. Getting them eighteen hundred and fifty feet away—the outdoor evacuation distance to protect them from flying debris from a bomb of this size— would be impossible.

Many of them would follow police orders and move far enough, fast enough. Those people would at least survive. The people in the store probably didn't have enough time to truly get clear, if the bomb worked as intended. At least some of them, plus the police officers helping people evacuate, would surely be killed.

Hand entry, manually rendering a bomb safe, was something he'd done in practice. It was even something he'd done out in the field, wearing his bomb suit. But it was dangerous in the best of conditions. With no time to fully evaluate the bomb before he made decisions, this was far from the best of conditions.

He trusted his gut, trusted his training. But this was the worst scenario, the one he'd never dreamed he'd face when he'd volunteered—no, *fought*—to become a bomb technician.

With an IED, it was all about interfering with the detonation or triggering system. But there were so many possible configurations, so many possible ways to detonate it during that process. Assessing the bomb was one of the most important steps. It determined everything else, from whether you tried to move it to how exactly you attempted to render it safe. Right now, that assessment would be cursory at best.

He tried to close everything from his mind except the bomb itself, all of the little clues about what might trigger it or disarm it. He could still hear Ava's voice, calm and focused, continuing to advise the Chief about the size and type of bomb, where she'd seen civilians, the closest exits and entrances.

His heart thundering in his ears, Eli evaluated how to access and disrupt the triggering system. Dennis had been smart, making it tricky to reach, tricky to tell for sure if there was a secondary trigger on it.

Twenty-seven seconds.

The world around him dimmed, even Ava's voice fading into nothing, as Eli fell back on his training. Those six weeks at the FBI's Hazardous Devices School, where he learned to use his robot, how to do a contained explosion and right now, most importantly, where he'd practiced disabling bombs in place. In practice, he'd worn a bomb suit. In practice, he'd had more than twenty-seven seconds.

Sliding his mirror along the inside of the black case, Eli searched for any sign of a second trigger tucked among the explosives. He didn't see one.

Twenty-two seconds.

His heart thundered, the loudest sound he could hear, as he selected a precision cutting tool from his case. It was an awkward fit, slipping his hand in sideways between the explosives and the case, to get to where the triggering device was positioned.

He slowed his breathing, relaxed his grip and slid the tool farther into the case, using his inspection mirror to guide him.

Seventeen seconds.

"Ava," he said, and immediately she was leaning closer. "Hold the mirror right here."

When she took it, he grabbed his spudger, a precision tool that let him separate small, sensitive components. He slid it in beside the cutting tool and used it to slide the wire he wanted away from the explosives slowly, to confirm the connection to the triggering device.

Nine seconds.

Easing the cutting tool up behind the trigger, he said a silent prayer and snipped.

Afterward, his heart continued to thunder in his ears, his gaze laser-focused on the triggering device.

Then, Ava's voice reached his ears, amazed and relived. "You did it. The timer turned off."

Letting out a breath, Eli slid his tools carefully away from the bomb. "Let's get the containment chamber down here to transport it safely."

He stood, and Ava squeezed his hand as she radioed up to the team, "It's safe. Eli disarmed the bomb."

She grinned at him as cheering filled the radio, and then individual voices started chiming in. First the Chief's, then Brady's and Jason's, then other members of the team. Congratulating him and Ava.

Her smile grew, the happiness in her eyes overshadowing the dirt and blood smeared across her uniform and her face, the snarled mess of her hair.

He could see it on her face. She finally, *finally* felt like part of the team.

But would it be enough to make her stay?

Epilogue

"Lacey!" A grin broke on Ava's face, far bigger than she could ever hope to contain, as the German shepherd came striding out of the back of the vet's office.

She wasn't moving with her usual speed or grace, but her tail was wagging.

Ava knelt in front of her and buried her head in the dog's long soft fur. Relief enveloped her. "I'm so glad you're okay, Lacey."

The dog nuzzled her head closer and Ava laughed. She didn't move until she heard Marie's voice.

"As you can tell, she's doing great."

Giving her dog one last pet, Ava stood. "Thank you for taking such good care of her."

"Of course. I'm happy she gets to go home today."

From the way Lacey's tail loudly thumped the ground, Ava thought she agreed.

"I'm glad you didn't need her yesterday," Marie continued. "I read in the paper this morning about the bomb that was disabled at the grand opening of Blaze's. I couldn't believe it. You were there?"

Ava nodded, thinking of those final moments beside

Eli, watching him work. Choosing to stand beside him, knowing he could save them all.

She'd been right. And it hadn't just been Eli who'd gotten a hero's reception when they climbed up from the basement. Her team had slapped her on the back, Jason kneeling to bandage her leg before an EMT could get through the crowd. Even Captain Rutledge had given her a genuine-looking smile, his tone heartfelt when he said, "Great job today, Officer Callan."

Somehow, she'd been pushed through the crowd of officers and civilians and put into an ambulance. They'd insisted she get checked out at the hospital. As the ambulance doors had closed, she'd seen Eli from a distance, heading back into the building with his bomb containment chamber. When her cuts and abrasions had been stitched up and debrided, and she'd finally been cleared by the doctor hours later, the Chief had told her to go home. He'd said Eli had already headed back to McCall.

Her heart pinched remembering it. Eli had left without even saying goodbye. Because he didn't want to bother her in case she'd gone home to sleep off the day, hell, the whole week? Or because he thought there was nothing left to say?

She'd been the one to change the tone at Millard's after her brother called. Maybe this was Eli trying to honor her wishes. But what had happened to pursuing her with all he had?

Shaking off the heavy disappointment weighing in her chest, Ava tried to smile as she told Marie, "I was there. I'm glad it's all over." She tried to mean it.

"Well, the department already paid for Lacey's care, so you're all set there. Here's her medicine." Marie handed her a small paper bag. "Call me if you have any questions or if Lacey doesn't continue to improve."

Ava must have looked worried, because Marie patted her arm. "Don't worry. She's doing great and I don't expect any setbacks. I wasn't kidding when I told you soon you'll be frustrated trying to limit her movements. She'll be back to a hundred percent before you know it."

"Thanks, Marie." On a whim, Ava leaned in and gave the vet a hug.

As Marie hugged her back, Ava thought about the call she'd missed that morning from Emma Daniels. The energetic K-9 ranch owner had left a long jumbled rush of a voice mail. How glad she was that Ava was okay, how she was looking forward to helping Lacey with any training she needed to get back up to speed, how one of these days Ava needed to stay for dinner with her and Tashya and whoever else was at the ranch.

She was making friends here. It wasn't the easy new start she'd expected and hoped for, but it was beginning to feel like home.

As she thanked Marie and headed for the door, Lacey at her side, Ava tried not to think about what was missing.

"Eli."

His name burst from her lips as soon as she stepped outside into the brilliant sunshine. She glanced at his side, taking in the enormous black dog beside him, tail wagging. Then her gaze rose back to his. "I thought you went home to McCall?"

"I did." He strode closer, his dog keeping pace, until he was right in front of her, those intense blue eyes she'd already missed in the past twenty-four hours focused solely on her.

Nervous excitement rose in her belly as she stared at him. From the corner of her eye, she watched Lacey stepping closer to the Newfoundland and the two dogs sniffing each other.

"Don't worry," Eli said, taking her hand.

She closed her hand around his tightly, hanging on, as he continued, "Bear is a gentle giant. He and Lacey will get along famously. That's why I went home. I needed to get some rest and wanted you two to meet Bear."

He grinned at her then and she couldn't help but smile back. Couldn't help but notice the nerves underneath his confident posture.

"I'm glad I made it back in time. I asked Marie when you were supposed to pick Lacey up, but you're a little bit early."

"You did?"

"Yeah." His thumb stroked the tops of her knuckles, making her nerve endings fire to life and her breathing become more shallow.

"I was hoping to bring you and Lacey back to my place for dinner. Or, if it's too far for Lacey to be in a car right now, maybe I can cook at your place?"

"You want to make me dinner?" Surprise and happiness burst inside of her and put some flirtation into her tone. "Is this step one of your plan to pursue me with everything you have?"

His grin grew wider. "You've got that right." It faded into something more serious as he added, "That is, if you're planning to stay in Jasper?"

Her smile turned tender at the fear and hope in his voice. "I do want to repair my relationship with my brother. I think it's going to happen, but it will take time. And I'm going to do it long distance, because Chicago just isn't where I belong anymore. Even though coming here wasn't quite as simple as I expected, there are things worth staying for." She touched her palm to his cheek, her voice dropping to a near-whisper. "There are *people* worth staying for."

Eli was worth staying for. It was early still, but he was special. Their connection was special.

She wasn't in a rush, but staring up at him now, just like when she'd first kissed him, she had that same certain feeling. Building a relationship with Eli wasn't just right; it was inevitable. And it was exactly what she wanted.

Woof!

A burst of laughter escaped as Ava glanced at Lacey, who had turned her head back toward her. She stroked Lacey's head gently, adding, "And there are dogs worth staying for, too, Lacey."

Appeased, Lacey turned back toward Bear, whose tail was wagging.

"I think you were right about them getting along," Ava said, her attention returning to Eli.

His expression was serious, intense, the grin nowhere in sight. "And you're worth pursuing with everything I've got, Ava Callen. So, get ready for some serious court-ship."

Then, that grin reappeared just long enough to make her heart flutter, before he dipped his head and kissed her.

* * * * *

K-9s on Patrol continues next month with

Foothills Field Search
by Maggie Wells.

*And if you missed
the first book in the series, look for*

Decoy Training
by New York Times *bestselling author*
Caridad Piñeiro

*Available now wherever
Harlequin Intrigue books are sold!*

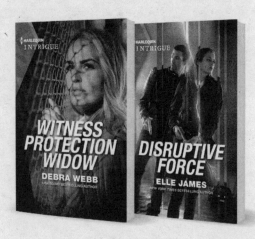

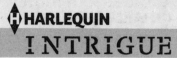
#2073 STICKING TO HER GUNS
A Colt Brothers Investigation • by B.J. Daniels

Tommy Colt is stunned when his childhood best friend—and love—
Bella Worthington abruptly announces she's engaged to their old-time nemesis!
Knowing her better than anyone, Tommy's convinced something is dangerously
wrong. Now Colt Brothers Investigations' newest partner is racing to uncover the
truth and ask Bella a certain question...if they survive.

#2074 FOOTHILLS FIELD SEARCH
K-9s on Patrol • by Maggie Wells

When two kids are kidnapped from plain sight, Officer Brady Nichols and his
intrepid canine, Winnie, spring into action. Single mother Cassie Whitaker thought
she'd left big-city peril behind—until it followed her to Jasper. But can Brady and
his K-9 protect Cassie from a stalker who won't take no for an answer?

#2075 NEWLYWED ASSIGNMENT
A Ree and Quint Novel • by Barb Han

Hardheaded ATF legend Quint Casey knows he's playing with fire asking
Agent Ree Sheppard to re-up as his undercover wife. To crack a ruthless Houston
weapons ring, they must keep the mission—and their explosive chemistry—under
control. But Quint's determined need for revenge and Ree's risky moves are
putting everything on the line...

#2076 UNDERCOVER RESCUE
A North Star Novel Series • by Nicole Helm

After the husband she thought was dead returns with revenge on his mind,
Veronica Shay resolves to confront her secret past—and her old boss,
Granger Macmillan, won't let her handle it on her own. But when they fall into a
nefarious trap, they'll call in their entire North Star family in order to stay alive...

#2077 COLD CASE CAPTIVE
The Saving Kelby Creek Series • by Tyler Anne Snell

Returning to Kelby Creek only intensifies Detective Lily Howard's guilt at the
choice she made years ago to rescue her childhood crush, Anthony Perez, rather
than pursue the man abducting his sister. But another teen girl's disappearance
offers a chance to work with Ant again—and a tantalizing new lead that could
mean inescapable danger.

#2078 THE HEART-SHAPED MURDERS
A West Coast Crime Story • by Denise N. Wheatley

Attacked and left with a partial heart-shaped symbol carved into her chest,
forensic investigator Lena Love finds leaving LA to return to her hometown comes
with its own danger—like detective David Hudson, the love she left behind.
But soon bodies—all marked with the killer's signature heart—are discovered in
David's jurisdiction...

*Wedding bells and shotgun fire are ringing out
in Lonesome, Montana. Read on for another
Colt Brothers Investigation novel from* New York Times
bestselling author B.J. Daniels.

Bella Worthington took a breath and, opening her eyes, finally faced her reflection in the full-length mirror. The wedding dress fit perfectly—just as he'd said it would. While accentuating her curves, the neckline was modest, the drape flattering. As much as she hated to admit it, Fitz had good taste.

The sapphire-and-diamond necklace he'd given her last night gleamed at her throat, bringing out the blue-green of her eyes—also like he'd said it would. He'd thought of everything—right down to the huge pear-shaped diamond engagement ring on her finger. All of it would be sold off before the ink dried on the marriage license—if she let it go that far.

As she studied her reflection, though, she realized this was exactly as he'd planned it. She looked the beautiful bride on her wedding day. No one would be the wiser.

She could hear music and the murmur of voices downstairs. He'd invited the whole town of Lonesome, Montana. She'd watched from the upstairs window as the guests had arrived earlier. He'd wanted an audience for this and now he would have one.

The knock at the door startled her, even though she'd been expecting it. "It's time," said a male voice on the other side. One of Fitz's hired bodyguards, Ronan, was waiting. He would be carrying a weapon under his suit. Security, she'd been told, to keep her safe. A lie.

She listened as Ronan unlocked her door and waited outside, his boss not taking any chances. He had made sure there was no possibility of escape short of shackling her to her bed. Fitz was determined that she find no way out of this. It didn't appear that she had.

In a few moments, she would be escorted downstairs to where her maid of honor and bridesmaids were waiting—all handpicked by her groom. If they'd questioned why they were down there and she was up here, they hadn't asked. He wasn't the kind of man women questioned. At least not more than once.

For another moment, Bella stared at the stranger in the mirror. She didn't have to wonder how she'd gotten to this point in her life. Unfortunately, she

HIEXP0322INC

knew too well. She'd just never thought Fitz would go this far. Her mistake. He, however, had no idea how far she was willing to go to make sure the wedding never happened.

Taking a breath, she picked up her bouquet from her favorite local flower shop. The bouquet had been a special order delivered earlier. Her hand barely trembled as she lifted the blossoms to her nose for a moment, taking in the sweet scent of the tiny white roses—also his choice. Carefully, she separated the tiny buds, afraid it wouldn't be there.

It took her a few moments to find the long, slim silver blade hidden among the roses and stems. The blade was sharp, and lethal if used correctly. She knew exactly how to use it. She slid it back into the bouquet out of sight. He wouldn't think to check it. She hoped. He'd anticipated her every move and attacked with one of his own. Did she really think he wouldn't be ready for anything?

Making sure the door was still closed, she checked her garter. What she'd tucked under it was still there, safe, at least for the moment.

Another knock at the door. Fitz would be getting impatient and no one wanted that. "Everyone's waiting," Ronan said, tension in his tone. If this didn't go as meticulously planned, there would be hell to pay from his boss. Something else they all knew.

She stepped to the door and opened it, lifting her chin and straightening her spine. Ronan's eyes swept over her with a lusty gaze, but he stepped back as if not all that sure of her. Clearly he'd been warned to be wary of her. Probably just as she'd been warned what would happen if she refused to come down—or worse, made a scene in front of the guests.

At the bottom of the stairs, the room opened and she saw Fitz waiting for her with the person he'd hired to officiate.

He was so confident that he'd backed her into a corner with no way out. He'd always underestimated her. Today would be no different. But he didn't know her as well as he thought. He'd held her prisoner, threatened her, forced her into this dress and this ruse.

But that didn't mean she was going to marry him.

She would kill him first.

Don't miss
Sticking to Her Guns *by B.J. Daniels,*
available June 2022 wherever
Harlequin books and ebooks are sold.

Harlequin.com

Get 4 FREE REWARDS!

We'll send you 2 FREE Books plus 2 FREE Mystery Gifts.

FREE
Value Over
$20

Both the **Harlequin Intrigue®** and **Harlequin® Romantic Suspense** series feature compelling novels filled with heart-racing action-packed romance that will keep you on the edge of your seat.

YES! Please send me 2 FREE novels from the Harlequin Intrigue or Harlequin Romantic Suspense series and my 2 FREE gifts (gifts are worth about $10 retail). After receiving them, if I don't wish to receive any more books, I can return the shipping statement marked "cancel." If I don't cancel, I will receive 6 brand-new Harlequin Intrigue Larger-Print books every month and be billed just $5.99 each in the U.S. or $6.49 each in Canada, a savings of at least 14% off the cover price or 4 brand-new Harlequin Romantic Suspense books every month and be billed just $4.99 each in the U.S. or $5.74 each in Canada, a savings of at least 13% off the cover price. It's quite a bargain! Shipping and handling is just 50¢ per book in the U.S. and $1.25 per book in Canada.* I understand that accepting the 2 free books and gifts places me under no obligation to buy anything. I can always return a shipment and cancel at any time. The free books and gifts are mine to keep no matter what I decide.

Choose one: ☐ **Harlequin Intrigue**
Larger-Print
(199/399 HDN GNXC)

☐ **Harlequin Romantic Suspense**
(240/340 HDN GNMZ)

Name (please print)

Address   Apt. #

City   State/Province   Zip/Postal Code

Email: Please check this box ☐ if you would like to receive newsletters and promotional emails from Harlequin Enterprises ULC and its affiliates. You can unsubscribe anytime.

Mail to the Harlequin Reader Service:
IN U.S.A.: P.O. Box 1341, Buffalo, NY 14240-8531
IN CANADA: P.O. Box 603, Fort Erie, Ontario L2A 5X3

Want to try 2 free books from another series! Call 1-800-873-8635 or visit www.ReaderService.com.

---

*Terms and prices subject to change without notice. Prices do not include sales taxes, which will be charged (if applicable) based on your state or country of residence. Canadian residents will be charged applicable taxes. Offer not valid in Quebec. This offer is limited to one order per household. Books received may not be as shown. Not valid for current subscribers to the Harlequin Intrigue or Harlequin Romantic Suspense series. All orders subject to approval. Credit or debit balances in a customer's account(s) may be offset by any other outstanding balance owed by or to the customer. Please allow 4 to 6 weeks for delivery. Offer available while quantities last.

Your Privacy—Your information is being collected by Harlequin Enterprises ULC, operating as Harlequin Reader Service. For a complete summary of the information we collect, how we use this information and to whom it is disclosed, please visit our privacy notice located at corporate.harlequin.com/privacy-notice. From time to time we may also exchange your personal information with reputable third parties. If you wish to opt out of this sharing of your personal information, please visit readerservice.com/consumerschoice or call 1-800-873-8635. **Notice to California Residents**—Under California law, you have specific rights to control and access your data. For more information on these rights and how to exercise them, visit corporate.harlequin.com/california-privacy.

HIHRS22